The Aftermath
Of
Love and War

A Novel

Mary McClurkin

The Aftermath of Love and War
Copyright © 2017 Mary McClurkin

ISBN-13: 978-1545203699
ISBN-10: 1545203695

First printing April 2017

Printed in the United States of America

Available in e-book.
Edited by Karen Rodgers

DEDICATION

This book has been a long time coming. For many years I toiled with writing it. Finally, I read in the Bible, Habakkuk 2-3, "And the LORD answered me, and said, Write the vision, and make it plain upon tables, that he may run that readeth it. ³ For the vision is yet for an appointed time, but at the end it shall speak, and not lie: though it tarry, wait for it; because it will surely come, it will not tarry. I began to write knowing at the appointed time, it would be published and would help those who needed hope and something to build their faith.

With gratitude, I say thanks to the many people whom I know I worked their nerves to no end. But you always had time for me. We have prayed together, cried together, at times laughed and acted silly to keep focused on writing and in finding common ground with you as writers, proofreaders, and those who selected the book cover. To all of you who helped, I'm grateful for the Holy Spirit who led me to you.

Thank you, Elder Jerry and wife Agnes, Anna Mae, Sylvia, Jessie Mae, and my spiritual advisor, Pastor Herbert Crump and Lady Dawn Crump, who stood right by my side praying for me and guiding me step-by-step. Please know you can relax now and stop wondering what will be next.

I dare not leave out my daughters, grandchildren and great grandchildren. You all went through something with me writing this book and at times you didn't want to see or hear from me. I must admit, I worked your nerves. But through it all, you know that Mama and grandma loves you guys more than herself.

Thanks to my prayer partner, Brenda. Thanks to the physicians whom I have worked with for many years. To my granddaughter, fashion model, Emma J., thank you for the beautiful picture on the cover. Your grace and charm will shine all around the world. To Brandon Zachery at BJZ Photography for the picture, thank you. You have a special gift. To Andrea Bostic, thank you for the graphics work.

To my editor, Karen Rodgers, thank you for your skills and patience. To author, K.T. Richey, thank you for being right there for me, helping me through this process and knowing exactly what I was going through. To Pastor Donnie McClurkin, thank you for not allowing me to give up. You pushed me to the limit.

If I have forgotten anyone, please know that I appreciate everything that you have done for me. All of you are great friends and family. To God be the Glory!

Mary McClurkin

Chapter 1

I WAS BORN in the woods in a small town not far from the state capital of South Carolina. It was a Sunday and my daddy, who was pastor of the local sanctified church, had left my mama at home so he could go to church and deliver his sermon. While he was gone, the midwife delivered me right on our front porch, the last of ten children, six boys and four girls. I don't know if the world was ready for Ella Mae Williams but I was ready for it. Mama told me I came out with my eyes wide open and screaming and hollering as if someone had awakened me out of a deep sleep.

"This one gon' be slick," the midwife told my mama. "Got her eyes wide open. Already looking for trouble." She cleaned me, wrapped me in a towel and placed me in my mother's arms.

I grew up in a scene that looked as if it were straight out of the movies, modest, but beautiful. Acres of land spread out so far, the land and horizon became one. Trees stretched upward toward the sky as if they were reaching toward heaven. The sounds of the farm animals by day and the crickets and frogs by night sang a peaceful harmony in the tranquil setting.

Our first house was six rooms built on a wooden frame, box style with a back porch. In our front yard was a giant oak tree planted in the reddest clay you can imagine, the kind that stuck to your ankles and pant legs when you walked through it. There was no paint on our walls or on the exterior, no electricity or running water; no luxuries of any kind. But, that house had more love in it than any mansion you see today.

We had a relationship with nature and with our land unlike today where the market and megastores house everything you would ever need. Because we had few resources of our own, we had to be creative with the resources that existed all around us. My mama, Bessie, was a housewife who used the land to do all those things women do to make their homes pretty. I remember one day, she took our curtains and a white bedspread that a white family from town had given to us and walked outside with them. I followed her and watched as she dug a hole in the clay and laid the curtains and bedspread inside. She covered the hole and watered it for a week to keep it muddy. The rain did the rest. I don't think you could find a shade of orange in a store that was prettier than those linens.

The children were more creative than the adults. The forest was our playground and it stretched out for acres and acres, just for us. As soon as I was old enough to play outside, I joined my brothers and sisters for hours of running and playing and yelling through those woods. We'd jump rope, play tag and compete with one another to see who could get their voice to echo the loudest through the trees. We never worried about criminals in the woods or people whipping us for being too loud. Our closest neighbors lived six miles away. Somehow, we managed to get ourselves into trouble anyhow.

One year, we built ourselves a playhouse from tree branches and feed sacks from the chicken coop. We were all very proud of it and spent lots of time in and around it. One of my sisters decided one day that she wanted to play house and thought it'd be a good idea to make a fire in the house for "cooking." Well, all it took was one spark to hit those feed sacks and the whole thing went up in flames. Everybody ran out as quickly as they could, except my sister. She got so scared that she went running back and forth from one side of the house to the other, just screaming. I stood back stunned as my brothers tried to pump water from the well as fast as they could. The small bucket of water they tossed on the fire did nothing to stop the rushing flames. Fortunately, my grandfather was close by and came running when he heard our screams and saw the flames. It was a sight: my grandfather yelling and putting out the flames and my sister still running back and forth until the whole thing just caved in. He grabbed the stick that propped up the house and whipped her behind good that day.

We had few neighbors, but lots of country legends, real and fake. One of the real ones was a hermit we called, "Pappy." The story around town was that Pappy was the only black man who lived in the State Park. The park rangers were afraid of him. We were too. We loved him, but like most country legends, fear was a big part of the love. None of us kids ever saw him. But people said that his skin was black as coal, but nobody was sure he was African-American. Many of the Native Americans that lived in the area had dark skin.

He lived in a makeshift home of branches, tin and whatever else he could get to keep the cold out in the winter and he ate from the forest: roots, berries, wild onion and anything the earth made that was edible. Other people said he was like a medicine man too; he knew all the plants and herbs in the forest and what they could cure. Still others claimed that he knew how to talk to animals and that the 'coons, deer and bobcats were his best friends. They also said that he had animal-like instincts and if you went looking for him, you'd never see him first because he could blend into nature like a chameleon and the snakes would protect him from you. My brothers and my dad believed that the park rangers left him food in the park on a regular basis. I didn't understand why he bothered with their food when he had his own. But they told me that every time the park rangers came back to where they'd left it, everything would be gone.

Our cows loved to graze near where Pappy lived. There was plenty of shade, sweet grass and clover and the state park had plenty of little streams running through it. One day, the cows wandered into the woods by themselves, and my brothers were afraid to go get them. My dad went and met Pappy standing near the edge of the woods. He told us later that Pappy was a jungle man and that we should never go bothering him because no one could be sure how he'd react. When Pappy died, they had to pull his body out of the marsh on a sled. My dad identified the body and recited the Lord's Prayer over him. If he had any family, nobody knew it. Daddy never told us where he was buried.

We were country folk living in a period that was post-slavery, but pre-civil rights. The land we first lived on was not ours; my parents were both sharecroppers and worked the fields behind the house with my brothers and sisters as field hands. There was never much to be gained from that kind of work: no income, no ownership, not even from the cotton, sugarcane, and food that we planted, tended and harvested. We did the work only to see the fruits of our labor shipped out to support the owner's family. When I turned fourteen years old, Mama had had enough. She demanded that we find another way to survive. And we were blessed. My daddy bought a piece of land about a mile from where we lived, across the street from a large white family. Daddy tore down the house on the land and together, we built a new house without a blueprint.

We worked just as hard as we played. Caring for a family of twelve was no easy task. Every day there were endless chores to be done around the house: cooking, cleaning, washing clothes, keeping the house warm. We were the only family in the community with a well, and that was one of our greatest assets. Neighbors, travelers, passersby, and the homeless all drew from our well and adults would talk about the latest news and gossip from around the town. Children, back then, were never part of grown folks' conversations, and so we'd play around or stand by quietly and pretend we weren't eavesdropping while our parents talked and talked, sometimes with complete strangers. People weren't so wary or suspicious of one another back then. And the conversations were more than just good social interactions; they were good manners.

Life was simpler then. Our wants were few, partly because our options were limited, but mostly because our priorities were different. There were no malls or discount outlets where black folks could spend time and money and even if there were, we wouldn't have been able to afford it. And women cooked for their families every day, so even if you could find a restaurant that served black folk, it was looked on as wasteful. At the time, there were two movie theaters in town and it was a very rare treat to be allowed to venture that far. I'd usually go when I was in town visiting my grandmother, who we called, "Ma Lil," and my cousins. The theater, like everything else, was segregated: white folk on the first floor and black folk in the balcony. And it was always hot, in every season. The air conditioner only served the first floor in the summer and the heater overpowered the theater in the winter, drenching us with sweat. Cars were a luxury that few could afford. Our family didn't own one until the late 1940s. My daddy would generally ride to the church with a neighbor who had a car and we children would get to and from places in whatever way we could manage: catching the bus, a mule-driven wagon, getting a free ride from the milkman, hopping on the bed of a wood hauler's truck, or just walking for miles. If a black family was fortunate enough to own a car, there was only one, and with very few exceptions, only the men drove. The only women I remember seeing in the driver's seat back then were teachers.

In so many ways, large families like mine were completely self-sufficient, because there was no other way to support ourselves. The children were each other's playmates and family was a source of love, encouragement and entertainment. I remember spending Sunday afternoons in our living room, all of us gathered around the organ that my mother played—our one luxury—and singing for the few minutes my mama had to spare before preparing our dinner. Her voice would carry farther than any one of ours and it was so beautiful that we'd beg for more time to listen and sing along. But there was always work to be done. We relished the time we had and moved forward to the next week.

The Williams were a tight-knit family for several reasons, but most importantly, I think, was the time in which we lived. For my generation, family was the most important aspect of any person's life. The only thing that was supposed to take greater priority was faith, and faith and family were always inseparable values. Our faith taught us how to be a family, and because my daddy was a minister, faith was our family. Minister's children were held to a different standard than other families; we were expected to set the example for the God-fearing members of our community. Our rules were more stringent; our parents were stricter than most. We all suffered lots of beatings because of these standards, especially me, but the purpose wasn't to be abusive. It was a commitment to keeping our family together and to keeping the children on the right track. I understand this now far better than I did then. If there was nothing else to be had in our home, there was always peace and order. And that's something never to be taken for granted.

I prayed for that kind of peace and order almost every day of my marriage. It never came.

Chapter 2

I KNEW THE DAY I saw Bill Anderson at the well, he was my husband. I was five years old. He was ten. His father had recently moved him and his brother and sister to town and the well beside our house was their closest water source. I remember that day very well, for no other reason than what I said when I saw him. My mama was going about her daily chores, and because I was only five, I went wherever she went. I took one look at this boy standing near me at the well with his brown eyes and long eyelashes with his hands shoved in the pockets of his pants that had a patch on the knee. His head was filled with soft thick curls that gave the appearance that his mama could have been white. He smiled and stared back at me and I had to resist the urge to run up to him and ask his name. Girls didn't do that sort of thing back then. He was too much for this little girl to handle. He was the prettiest thing I had ever seen. I said loud enough for my mama to hear, "Ohhh, that boy is good lookin'. That's the one I'm gonna marry." Mama snatched me by my arm and whipped my butt right then and there, right in front of him. I was being way too "fast" for a little girl. But, back in those days, most anything a girl would do or say was considered "fast."

Around the time I met Anderson, America had just entered World War II. My oldest brother went off to fight. We called him, "Bye." I'm not sure why. Mama prayed every day for him and he made it back home.

There was an army training camp near our home and I remember the soldiers setting up their living barracks in the woods around our house. We'd see them just about every day, walking through town, or driving their tanks through the woods, sending us running off in terror. The women of Paw Creek were very wary of the soldiers and spent a good amount of time instilling fear into everyone who would listen. Ma Lil, my maternal grandmother was a midwife, and she'd travel around from house to house, catching stories and bits of gossip at every stop.

"Velma, don't let those girls out your sight," she'd tell my mama. "These soldiers is raping those young girls."

Mama was cautious, of course, but my family had a different opinion of the soldiers. To us they were heroes, in more ways than one. We opened our home to them whenever they traveled along our road. They would come in to get warm and Mama would cook and clean for them. That was patriotism. We were good to them and in the end, they were very good to us.

Winter is always a difficult time for a country family and even more difficult during a war. I was about six years old and my Mama canned and stored up food, as usual, but my parents soon realized that it wasn't enough to get us through the season. At the time, the nation was undergoing a food shortage. There was no work. We felt it hard in our grocery stores and in our pantries. Our situation would've been far more difficult had the soldiers not helped us. Under martial law, any leftover food rations were required to be destroyed on site; no resources could be shared with civilians. In fact, the soldiers weren't really supposed to have any interaction with civilians, unless it was directly related to their specific assignments.

The soldiers knew of our needs, mostly because of their interactions with us, but were legally bound against giving us their extra rations. So, they didn't share them. They left them behind—burying them about a mile from our house with a wooden cross marking the spot—and moved on. The looks on my parents' faces when they pulled the food from the hole must have been priceless. There was ham, potatoes, beans, rice, cooking oil and sugar, and more than enough to hold us through the winter.

All those soldiers who had been so good to us had not yet experienced war. I don't know what happened to any of them, but I'm certain that they returned—if they survived— as very different men, just as my brother did. I couldn't imagine at the time that Anderson could be anything but the hero that each one of those soldiers was when I was little.

Anderson was never fond of school. I always said he only went to mess around with the girls. My brothers were around his age and quickly became friends with him. But it seemed like they passed him in school just as quickly. By the time he enlisted in the army, he'd barely made it to high school and I had just made it into the seventh grade. He finished his high school education while he was in basic training.

My mama decided early on that she wanted her daughters to be educated before they were married. She took pride in all the work she did for us and in the house, but she didn't want her daughters to be limited to housework. That wasn't progress. She was determined that we would go beyond what she had done, so that living would be easier for us and for her grandchildren. In addition to being restricted by religion and the social customs of our time, the Williams girls were also restricted by progress in our interactions with the opposite sex.

Ideas about a woman's place in society were changing. Tradition was being challenged by traditional women like my mama, who saw what a few women had managed to accomplish in profession and in independence, and realized that it was possible for a woman to go further, to do more than keep the house and the children. And if it wasn't possible for them, they would make it possible for those who came after them.

The most revered women in our community, by men and women alike, were those who had managed to obtain an education beyond high school and enter a profession. Most women professionals of that era were teachers. We would see them in town, sitting behind the wheel of their own cars, dressed in professional clothing. Most of them were unmarried, which went over well with some and not so well with others. But whatever your opinion of them, they were too unique not to notice.

At the same time, traditional roles remained just as strict for uneducated women and women who chose to be housekeepers and housewives. The man was the ruler—that was one of the first things we all learned. Even though my mama expected her daughters to go further than she did, she still made sure we knew our "place" at home. She would make sure that we knew to always do what the man said and she demonstrated this in the way that she obeyed my daddy. He was a very quiet man, but he never had to say much because it was always understood that we followed his commands. There was never a choice to say no. The girls all observed this and knew that there was nothing that could be done about it. In the home, a woman was an adult child. If she voiced her opinion, the husband would say, "Who's the head? I'm the one supposed to look out for you. You can't tell me what's best." And because that was the norm, because we didn't know that it could be any different, we accepted this place, no matter how bad that place was for us.

When I was thirteen years old, my eighteen-year-old sister, the third girl of the family, had her first child—out of wedlock. My grandfather whipped her for disgracing his family and my daddy's position as the moral leader of the community. Mama would tolerate no more mishaps. And from that moment until I was engaged, I was on lock-down. No courting, no dating, and no wearing anything that would mark me as accessible to any man. That meant no makeup, large earrings, and no stockings until I graduated high school.

I fought it in whatever way I could. I never wanted to be a housewife like my mama, but I did want to be married and have lots of children, just as she did. I was a typical teenager for the time; rebellious but grounded, if only because I was always being watched by everyone, especially people who knew Mama or Ma Lil. There wasn't very much anybody could get away with in those days. I remember mornings when I would leave the house looking very much like the nice, conservative little girl my mama wanted me to be, only to transform into a "grown" woman before my first class at school. A friend of mine who, like me, wasn't allowed to wear big earrings, decided to get creative. She made earrings for me, herself, and some of our other friends out of the crystals from a chandelier in her dining room. We'd put them on with some lipstick and stay made up until the end of the school day, when we'd go into the bathroom and carefully remove all traces of the lipstick from our mouths and hand the earrings back to her so we could do it all over again the next day. Of course, I got caught. One of Ma Lil's friends told her that she'd seen me wearing lipstick and the crystals, and I got beat for being "fast."

My career path was also limited to what was "morally" acceptable by faith and family. I used to sing in school and there was a talent scout who wanted to take me to New York for an audition. Mama refused. Back then, the non-secular music scene was associated with drugs, sex and "the fast life." "Ain't no devil gonna get my child," she said. And that was the end of it.

The same applied to sports. I wanted to play for the girls' basketball team in high school, but it wasn't allowed because it meant that I would have to wear shorts. That was too progressive. Women in my town didn't even wear pants then.

"You want the men folk to see your legs, huh?" she said to me. And that was the end of that.

But Bill Anderson was far more important than earrings or makeup or even singing and basketball. He smiled all the time. He was very mature and respectful to his elders. He liked to wear a shirt with a lay back collar so it could be laid outside his sport jacket. His shirt was always very white with no wrinkles. He would unbutton three buttons down from the collar so the hair on his chest would show. He was very hairy. He wore his hair parted on the right side. He kept his hands in his pockets at all times except when he would smoke a cigar or cigarette. One day when he and my brothers were picking peaches, he told my brothers that he was going to marry me. My brother came home and told my mama and I got a whipping because Mama thought that I had to have been seeing him behind her back. She was right. But, it wasn't the way she thought; the truth didn't matter. And I was so thrilled when I heard what he said, the beating didn't matter. I would take a beating for him any day.

One day he sent me a note. My friend Irene gave it to me at school. He wanted me to meet him down at the creek, behind the school, near the rocks. It was our secret meeting place; one where we couldn't be seen and I could get in and out of without being noticed. I arrived five minutes after the school bell sounded. I still wore my chandelier earrings and made sure my cheeks were pink and lips had an extra layer of lipstick.

I rushed through the woods until I saw him standing near the creek bed throwing rocks into the calm waters. He turned when he heard my footsteps. The biggest smile crossed his face showing his deep dimples. My heart melted each time I saw him.

"You know your mama gon' get you with all that stuff on your face." He laughed and walked to me. "You too pretty to be wearing all that stuff anyway."

I blushed and hugged him. He smelled of fresh cut wood from the sawmill down the street where he worked.

"My mama don't hafta know my business," I said with fake bravado.

He slid his hands in the pockets of the pleated pants he wore and looked down at the ground. His shoes were so shiny as if he'd freshened them up for me.

A chipmunk caught my attention as it scurried through the thick brush. "What you call me down here for?" I asked him.

"I wanted to tell you I signed up for the army. I'm leaving in the morning."

"Whatcha go do a fool thing like that for?"

"I was thinking about my future ... our future. Man can't make no living down here in the po' country. You either a sharecropper or work in the lumber yard. Man can't take care of his family like that."

My heart skipped as I listened to him talking about taking care of his family. I felt right then and there he was going to ask me to marry him. My chest hurt; I couldn't breathe.

He gripped my shoulders. "I love you and I want to get both of us out of this town. Ain't nothing here for us. In the army, I can learn a trade. The pay is good and I can save up enough money to show your daddy and Mama I can take care of you." He released me. "I'm doing this for us." He looked so sincere. It was the most romantic thing he ever said to me.

I thought at that moment I was going to faint. "What am I gon' do when you leave?"

"I'll write you every day. I promise. It won't be long."

He wrapped his arms around me and held me close. I wanted to give my all to him. The good men in those days respected women like he showed me by releasing me and saying, "You better go on now. Yo' mama be awfully mad if you late from school."

I started to run back but I turned to him, "I'll write you every day too."

He grinned.

I started to leave but I heard him call my name.

"Ella Mae," he said and pointed to his earlobes reminding me I still had the earrings in my ear.

I quickly took them off and shoved them in my pocket and ran back toward the school full of hope and promise.

We started courting as soon as he left for the military. Courting was different back then. We didn't go to movies or restaurants. He was away serving our country and I wrote to him almost every day. It wasn't easy getting that past my mama. She watched me like a hawk. I had to have a courier. I'd find two cents somewhere for each letter, sneak the letters out the house on my way to school in the morning and pass them on to one of my friends who lived in town. Mama never knew that I wrote to him. But of course, she read every letter he wrote to me.

Children weren't allowed to fetch the mail. That was grown folks' business. And so, I never got to read all the letters he wrote, because my mama withheld the ones she thought were inappropriate. She would read all my letters and cut out parts before she gave them to me. I had to use my imagination to fill in the blanks not knowing what was said. My mother felt as if I was being too grown. Back then, they called it being manish. It was frustrating, but I was grateful that she allowed me to read any of them. They were lost in a fire years ago, but what I do remember of them was the romance. One I remember he said he couldn't wait to get back home. The rest was cut out. I could only imagine that he wanted to see me, to hold me in his arms and kiss me until I forgot my name. I wanted the same.

He was charming. And it was even more romantic that he'd waited as long as he did to court me and that he spent his free time writing to me. When he was on tour in Germany, he sent me a beautiful gown and a box of perfume. Mama was furious.

"Bill Anderson is a man and there ain't but one woman in this house," she said. "Why he send you a gown? That means he wants to see you in it," she said.

She beat me that day and threw the gown into the fireplace. I cried and cried, but she wouldn't budge. I didn't get the perfume back until after I was married.

∞

He finally proposed to me in the spring of 1955, just before I graduated from high school. He sent me a note and I met him at the creek bed. He was in his dress green uniform which made him look taller and royal. He held a bouquet of fresh picked daisies in his hands. He looked nervous when he saw me.

"I didn't know you was coming home," I said to him.

"I wanted to surprise you." He held out the flowers to me. "I got these for you."

I took them and inhaled the pungent smell but that day I couldn't tell if they were daisies or roses. It was so sweet to me.

"I only have a couple days. This evening I'm gon' tell your daddy and mama we gone get married."

I gasped. Fear and excitement flooded my whole body. "Do you think that's a good idea? I ain't even graduated yet."

"You will soon and we gone get married. I ain't waiting no more. I got money saved. We can live on the base. I can't stand the thought of you being in this podunk town."

I wanted to leave just as badly as he wanted to take me away. But my body shook in anticipation of his arrival at six o'clock.

I bolted for my bedroom door as soon as I heard the knock. I peeped out to see my daddy answer the front door. He pulled it open and Anderson stood in front of him still in his dress greens. They shook hands and my daddy walked outside.

I don't know what was said, but my daddy came back in with a pained look on his face. He called for me and my mama. I walked into the room careful not to stare at Anderson or my daddy. I sat on the piano bench. My mama and daddy sat on the sofa. Anderson sat in the big chair that was reserved for Daddy when he counseled somebody in the church.

"I'll do right by Ella Mae," he assured my parents.

My mama gave me the evil eye as if she had just received confirmation of her suspicions.

My daddy reluctantly gave his approval with the condition I graduate first.

Anderson left. There were no hugs or kisses. No promises of eternal love and no ring.

After Mama found that out, she started letting me read his letters. I suppose she'd given up hope that I'd follow her plan for me. And in that case, there was nothing more to do than to validate our relationship before God.

Chapter 3

NEW YORK was forbidden.

Like all things my mama associated with sin and worldliness, New York was not for her daughter. When I graduated from high school, Anderson was off on an army tour in Germany and there was a year left before I was to marry. The town of Paw Creek was a dead-end place for a young woman like me; there was nothing to do but clean white people's houses which I hated. I plotted my escape.

As if the gods was looking over me, my brother announced he was getting married to a woman he met in New York. I was so excited it took everything in me to contain my desire...my *need* to go to the wedding. My brother had moved to New York some years before and was going to be married in June. Mama still didn't want me to go, not even for his wedding. I went to my sister and told her what I wanted to do.

"You let me handle Mama," she told me, understanding how easy it was to get stuck in the traditions of the Jim Crow South. "You got to get out of this town and see the world," she huffed. She placed her hands on her hips. "I don't know why it's okay for a man to leave and go somewhere to have a better living but a woman can't. All they want us to do is cook, clean, have babies and be some man's slave. Don't you worry. You going to that wedding."

It took some doing but she convinced Mama I was only going to be in New York for the wedding and vowed that she would look after me for that time. From the time that I boarded the train for New York City, until I returned to Paw Creek for my own wedding, Mama thought that I was coming right back home. My sister was the scapegoat and took my parents' criticism for me.

New York City in 1956 was just as vibrant and bustling and energetic as it is now. In Harlem, where I lived with a relative, there was the Palms Café, the Cotton Club and of course, the Apollo Theatre, where I went faithfully every week to the amateur shows and gospel hours. Walking through Harlem on any given day was like navigating a giant crowd of church folk after Sunday service. Women wore well-tailored skirts and dresses and blouses with sling backs or mules or wedge heels. Men strutted through the city in three-piece suits, bebop caps, and shiny penny loafers. The poor looked polished and the wealthy glowed. I'd never seen so many black folks living so well. That was the first time I realized just how poor my family was.

My mama was a laundress for a large white family in Paw Creek and she earned five cents for every shirt she ironed. There were no washing machines, no dryers and an iron was something you heated on the stove and hoped it wouldn't burn a hole through the more delicate garments. With all the work she had to do in her own house, it would sometimes take an entire day to finish one load. And it wasn't unusual for the family to "pay" her with leftover food from their dinner the night before rather than with money. When she would try to protest, they would say, "Oh Annie, (white folk always used the name "Annie" to refer to black women) we know you have all those children to feed. The food will be worth more to you than the money." She'd leave their home dignified, carrying leftovers and a new load of dirty laundry. But as soon as she walked through the door, we'd see the tears and know that she'd been cheated again. And there was nothing we could do.

New York was different. Women had choices there. If you chose to work for a white family, you could do so knowing that in most cases, you would not be expected to keep the house, cook and care for the children. Northern whites could afford to hire cooks, nannies, chauffeurs, and gardeners. The word "housekeeper" meant exactly what it said. "Housekeeper" back home meant that you kept everything that existed in and around the house: the children, the pets, the laundry, the meals, the dishes, the floors, the bathrooms, and the bedrooms. All of it was done by one black woman who almost always had her own house to keep and about five or six of her own children to feed and rear. And she'd do it for eight to ten dollars a week, enough to get by, but never enough to get ahead. Just one of those jobs in New York paid fifteen dollars a day. Life was more expensive there, but the pay was enough to live on and you didn't collapse at the end of the day.

I was never much for keeping anybody's house but my own and I wanted it to stay that way, for good reason. Back when I was about fifteen or sixteen, one of my relatives asked me to take over working at this white lady's house. She had gotten a job up north, and thought she should keep that job in the family. It was good pay back then, seventy-five cents for five hours of house cleaning on Saturdays. I jumped at the chance and showed up at the lady's house, ready to make some money. One of my chores was to mop her floor, which I thought was just filthy. It had all these brown, grey, and white speckles all over it. I went to work for a couple hours trying to clean that floor. I scrubbed it hard with Ajax and bleach, but none of the dirt seemed to come out.

Suddenly, the floor started to peel up all over, like little blisters. When that white lady came back in the house and saw that floor, she let out a big yell and fainted right there. The groceries she held rolled all over the kitchen floor. I ran next door to get her neighbor to help, and when she saw the floor, she gasped and covered her mouth.

"Honey, did you mop the floor?" the neighbor asked.

"Yessum!" I said, so proud of myself. I'd never scrubbed that hard in my life.

Trouble was, the specks on the floor weren't dirt. The floor was marble. I'd never seen anything like it before. When the woman finally came to, she told me to get out of her house and to never come back.

"Get out of my sight!" she screamed. "They came all the way from Columbia just to wax my floor and now look. You've messed it up for good."

I ran fast as I could to Ma Lil's house, which was two blocks away on the other side of the tracks, my heart in my mouth. That was the last time I cleaned for anybody.

In New York, I chose to work in a jewelry factory, making cufflinks and rings. I would keep about twenty dollars of every paycheck—enough for rent and for me—and I would send the rest to my mama, who was raising five grandchildren at home. My dad was torn about whether they should accept my money. He had a revival each week during July and August—black folk called it the "Big Meeting"—but it seemed like the extra money was never enough, and there were no jobs for colored folk in mills, stores or banks, any of the places where they could possibly get ahead. He appreciated the extra help, but he was still the man, and didn't want any confusion over who provided for his family.

"Baby," he wrote in one of his letters, "you act like I don't take good enough care of your mama. We're doing fine. Stop sending all of your money." Much as I valued his pride, I wasn't going to let my mama cry over another white folk's dime. I kept on sending the checks to them until I left New York.

For as much as the city had to offer and as much as I'd wanted to get out of the South, I wasn't prepared for the homesickness. I was a fish out of water, an eighteen-year-old country girl looking for home in a different world. There was no clay, no giant oaks, no animals to tend, no forest to explore, no fireplace, no schoolhouse, no truck to hop and no quiet. I was lost in concrete, metal and new manners. I cried day and night for two weeks until there was nothing left but acceptance and work. I worked Monday through Friday, and spent Saturday and Sunday at church or at the Apollo Theatre. I never dared go to the Cotton Club or Palm's Café— Mama called them "bear houses," places of ill repute where good girls didn't go.

At home, entertainment for black folk meant riding into town on the back of pulpwood trucks, wagons and milk trucks on Saturday, hanging out in the Back Lot, a local gathering spot, drinking and fighting, courting and dancing from sun up to sun down in the little makeshift building where they sold fried fish, hamburgers, hot dogs, chicken, pork chops, soft drinks, moonshine and Gulley rum whiskey made from homemade liquor. The men bragged about how much pulpwood they sold, and the women bragged about how much their white folks paid them. They played the banjo and harmonica on their trucks when the money ran out on the piccolo jukebox. And when the police came and beat the men or threw them in jail for "disturbing the peace," they'd take their punishment and they'd be right back in the Back Lot the next Saturday like a swarm of fire ants, to do it all over again. Those were the country folk I knew and loved. Slow paced, lively and happy.

City folk took some getting used to. The pace and culture made people act differently, even though many were raised in the South or had family living there. People moved so quickly through the streets, sometimes you'd think the concrete was burning their feet. They were less patient, and seemed to have less time than we had at home. It was rare that you were greeted on the sidewalk by a stranger, and if you ran into a friend or acquaintance, there was no time to stop and talk, no time to ask about the family and business. The world of New York was bigger, faster and busier, and my small-town ways didn't quite fit in anywhere except church. Canaan Baptist Church was where I found my friends and a place like home. You could find me at church six days out of seven. And by and by, as my church friends introduced me to their New York, I began to love the city as they did. New York was freedom. I obeyed the rules at home, but I was grown. Free to come and go as I pleased, free to discover me. Free from censorship. And free from indignity.

Paw Creek always considered itself above the atrocity of the Deep South, but remained fully committed to keeping us in our place. Jim Crow laws were still in effect by the time I moved to New York and as much as I loved home, I did not care to return to the mentality and confinement of segregation. I never dealt with it gracefully. At home, Jim Crow stalked me wherever I went; to the school yard and the courthouse, the corner store and the bakery. It followed me from the movie theater to the water fountain, from the toilet to the streets. Rule was, you were to give white people the right of way on any walking path, stepping down into the street when they passed, no matter what your age or condition. They reveled in it, enforcing it by intimidation or even violence whenever they felt it was necessary, and often when it was not.

I minded these rules consistently like most black folk. We opted for peace as often as possible. But there was only so much offense you could take on top of being forced to follow rules that lowered you to the status of an animal. One day a white couple, holding their baby, insulted my friend and me after we obediently stepped down into the street to let them pass; I snapped.

"You better have stepped in that street, nigger," the husband yelled at me, a smirk on his face.

That was South Carolina. The burn of indignity hit us every time we obeyed a law that made us inhuman. And though we didn't live in terror as others did, white folk always found ways of pouring salt into a wound, always reinforcing what we already knew; they had the power.

But on that day, and at that moment, I decided to take some power back, even if it was only temporary.

I snatched the baby out of his mother's hands, fuming as I faced them. My voice trembled, but my message was clear; they were going to apologize, or I couldn't be responsible for what happened to their baby. At sixteen, I wasn't fully aware of what could happen, and in some places, regularly did happen to blacks who confronted white folk, much less threatened their children. I don't think it would've mattered very much if I was.

We stood at a standstill for a few seconds. The mother's eyes were as wide as saucers and filled with something I hadn't seen often in white folks' eyes, but that I longed for at that moment: helplessness. For once, I wanted them to feel something like what my mama felt every time we crossed Jim Crow, even when we didn't know any better.

They mumbled something that sounded like an apology and took the baby from my arms. I got the beating of my life when I got home—there were eyes everywhere watching, ready to report back to your parents any misdeeds—but I wouldn't have changed a thing. On that day and at that moment, I won.

Jim Crow wasn't strictly a southern practice, but I never witnessed it in New York. I don't recall there ever being a place where I couldn't enter because of the color of my skin except for Coney Island. I lived in a neighborhood with black, white, Hispanic, and Asian people and everyone socialized together to some extent. Men were men and women were women. There were black folk working in just about every industry and profession you could imagine. There were black doctors, black lawyers, and black policemen. Those were jobs most of us only dreamed about in the South. The most challenging adjustment for me was simply getting rid of my old South mentality. I had to get used to being looked at as a valuable human being, a true citizen of my country. No more scrambling out of white folks' paths, no more eating in the backs of restaurants, no more segregated friendships. No more Annie. No more Uncle. No more until I had to go back home.

I let Anderson know I had moved to New York. Now I had the freedom to court him as I wished but there were no phone calls or visits, only letters. I was always excited to see that stamp on the envelope showing that it had come from overseas. My sister always placed them on the chifforobe for me to read when I got home.

They always started, *My dearest Ella Mae*. I couldn't wait to read the rest. I'd close my bedroom door blocking out anything that would draw my attention away from the words that I longed to hear.

> *My dearest Ella Mae. It has been days since I had time to write. Our sergeant has been very hard on us lately. We continue to persevere, completing every task. But at night my heart aches for you. My soul searches for the day you become my wife and we can be as one. I know you are in the big city and temptation is all around. Please remember my heart and count the days when we can be together again. We will be together soon.*
>
> *With love always, Bill*

I held the letters to my heart, hoping to feel the beat of his. I pushed the letter in the envelope and placed it with the others in the top drawer of the chifforobe. On lonely nights, I pulled out the small box holding my precious gift and read every one of them dreaming of the day I would become his wife.

Still I was young and as Anderson said, temptation was all around. I had three or four boyfriends but none of them compared to Anderson. Woodrow Miller came in a close second.

I met Woodrow at church. He was tall and slender and had a voice that could only be compared to the smooth rich voice of Sam Cooke. He sang on the choir with me. His parents had migrated from North Carolina to Harlem. In Harlem during that time, so many people had migrated from the South, if you asked anyone, they would tell you they were from the Carolinas, Georgia, or Florida. Everybody came to escape the oppression of the Deep South with expectation of a better life. Woodrow was born in Harlem. The South was only what he had heard from stories told by his elders and infrequent visits for reunions and funerals.

He was charming. "What a country girl like you doing up here in Harlem?" he asked me the first time we met. He had a habit of making fun of my southern drawl without insulting me.

My friends at church would tell me he was interested in me but I didn't pay him any attention; he wasn't Anderson. One day, after choir rehearsal, he walked me home. We talked along the way.

"You like it up here?" he asked, while walking backwards in front of me. He weaved in and out of the crowd as if he were born with eyes in the back of his head.

"I love it. Sometimes I miss my family." I tried to hide my interest but he seemed to pick up on it.

He smiled. "I'm gonna make sure you feel at home here. You can have family here too. Black folk can do real good up here. Ain't no sharecropping around here."

He was right about that. I was making more money than both of my parents. I had fancy clothes. I could go wherever I pleased without being treated like a second-class citizen. "What you do anyway?" I never knew how he earned his money. He was always dressed sharp in his suits and two-toned shoes. Even when he dressed casually in his pleated pants and oxford shirt, he looked like he was going to an important meeting at the church.

"I deliver liquor to the stores in town."

I tried to hold back my shock. He was not somebody my mama would approve of. He must have noticed the shock on my face because he laughed so loud it returned joy to my spirit. "Is that alright with you?"

"I have to say I was surprised. I guess it's okay if it's legal."

Many days we would sit on the stoop of my apartment and he would sing to me songs like the Platters, "Only You" and Roy Hamilton's, "Unchained Melody." He would snap his fingers and sing Ray Charles', "I Got a Woman." He would have people dancing on the sidewalk. He didn't need any instruments; his voice was all he required. Then on Sunday morning he would wake the church up with Clara Wards', "The Old Landmark."

It was easy to fall into his charms. We had fun together. On the weekends, he would show me around New York. The city had some of the tallest buildings I had ever seen. I stretched my neck trying to see the tops of the Singer Building, the Hudson Terminal and the St. Paul Building. When Coney Island was finally segregated, Woodrow took me to the park where we shared ice cream and rode rides that made my head spin.

To everyone else, we were a couple. To me he was just a friend, someone to ease the pain of the lonely days waiting for Anderson's return. To him I was the love of his life, at least that's what he said when he proposed to me. He gave me a simple ring. Looked like it came from the dime store. I know he worked hard for the money to purchase it but my heart belonged to Anderson. The disappointment on his face as he walked away broke my heart. I didn't mean to hurt him. I never lied to him about Anderson. I thought he understood we were only friends and I only wanted Anderson.

Right after my nineteenth birthday, I returned to Paw Creek. My mama was happy to see me but was disappointed it took me so long to return. I always felt she was upset that my sister and I betrayed her trust, but she never said it outright. Instead, she busied herself preparing for the wedding.

I was married on Fellowship day, a day when people from other churches around the county visited my daddy's church. It was the fifth Sunday.

Our wedding was simple, no bridesmaids or groomsmen. We held it in the front yard of my parents' house at 4:00 p.m., right after church. It was a beautiful spring day. The sky was the shade of blue that hinted of love and romance as wisps of clouds slowly drifted by. It was the perfect temperature and the early bugs had not awakened from their winter sleep. Sixty-five degrees and the yellow bells and pink azaleas were blooming across the lawn. There were wooden chairs lined up on the grass, just like at a concert, and when we ran out of those, our neighbor put his chair out near the preacher, and told everyone to "ring around" him.

I don't remember exactly how many people were there, but there were no formal invitations. Like everything else in that town, news about the wedding traveled by word of mouth. Most folk just headed right over to the house after the church service that day. The roadside was packed with old trucks and long cars, all parked just a few hundred yards from the well where I'd first met Anderson thirteen years before.

Forever the army man, he insisted on wearing his uniform, greenish brown and sharply pressed, his shoes shining like ice water. I was dressed in a white crinoline gown from Bloomingdale's NYC. There was a veil, but no train. It was the fanciest clothing I'd ever worn, and I felt beautiful, as every bride should. We had first kissed Friday before the wedding when he picked me up from the train station. He unceremoniously gave me my engagement ring then. It was simple like the one Woodrow tried to give me. But this one was special because Anderson picked it out himself. I made Anderson's wedding band myself at the jewelry factory in New York where I worked. It was a simple gold band, and I was proud of it because it was something I'd designed and crafted with my own hands. I thought it'd mean more to him than something from a jewelry store, but he was not a sentimental man.

The ceremony itself was everything I'd hoped for. I was surrounded by the people who'd helped to raise me, the people who loved me and knew me best. And I was marrying the love of my life. Anderson's family did not attend the wedding. His father died shortly after he joined the army, his brother was on duty in the army, and his sister simply didn't show up. I don't know why, but I do know that his sister didn't like me very much. But I didn't let any of that overshadow the joy of that moment. Nothing could stop my excitement for the wedding cake, the dancing, the food and the celebrating. Nothing of course, until he did.

We were signing the marriage license when he told me he was leaving for Oklahoma in a few days. He was going to be stationed at Fort Sill, and needed to report there immediately. He'd known this for a while.

"Why didn't you tell me earlier?" I asked. "I could've been packing."

"You'll have plenty of time to do that, but I got to go now. I'll be back for you as soon as I find a place for us," he said. "But right now, I want you to myself, so let's go. You can celebrate after I leave."

I convinced him to stay long enough to greet our guests and cut the cake. He complained of his hand hurting from shaking the hands of our many guests. My daddy was a popular preacher and several people came because of him, not that they knew either one of us. Either way, they wished us well.

We left my parents' house as it got dark by the lamplight; I followed him to his '55 Buick and sat in the passenger seat. I was nervous. My mama brought us a plate of food all wrapped up in a brown bag. She hugged me and shut the door.

Anderson looked at me and grinned. "You Mrs. Bill Anderson. I got you now."

We drove to his brother's house in silence, just married. There were no wedding bells.

∞

I knew what we were going to do. I'd been dreaming about it, imagining what I'd think and feel, what would come before and after. I'd imagined myself in the gown I chose for my honeymoon, having a quiet dinner before, with candlelight and cider. Of course, having no sense of these things, I made of it what I could. It felt romantic, because Anderson was the man of my dreams. He had charisma that made my heart stop even if he did nothing more than rip my wedding gown from me. My imagination was fed by watching happy marriages of family and friends that fueled what I thought would be the beginning of my perfect life.

"I've been waiting a long time to do this to you, Mrs. Bill Anderson," he said.

I liked the way that sounded.

"No more Ella Mae," I replied, grinning. "I'm Mrs. Bill Anderson now."

No more talk from there. Sweet whispers of love were the only sounds made. Not knowing what to expect, Anderson felt rough and unskilled the first time. The sting of lost virginity was discomforting and without pleasure. I knew he had been with many women. I had heard rumors. I guess I expected more. I wanted to be different than any other woman he had slept with.

When we were school children, he used to tell me he liked me because he knew I hadn't been running around with any other man.

"Your mama won't even let you look out the window after dark," he said. "And if you did, your brothers would tell it." To this day, I wonder what he was saving me for, if I was nothing special from the beginning.

It was after dark when we finished the second time. I was hungry. I wanted to be with my family, my friends. I wanted the night to end as it had in my head, crinoline swaying to slow music, laughter, kisses and hugs and tearful well wishes. A full stomach from the food my mama had slaved over for days.

"Anderson," I pleaded, "let's eat something." I didn't seem to have sense enough to rise and get the food myself. I guess I was waiting on him to tell me what to do.

"Tomorrow morning," he promised.

We must've woken up at about the same time the next morning because there was more sex. We spent most of our time in bed those first couple days, as most newlyweds do. When we finally did get out of bed, there wasn't much in the cabinets, and we were starving. The food we had was spoiled. We decided on grits. There was bacon and loaf bread in the fridge as well, and I wanted to make him breakfast, wanted to show off how good I was in the kitchen.

Even in the late fifties, a woman's worth to a man was still measured in large part by her ability to cook. I learned that lesson the hard way with Anderson later, but for the time being, he was a different man. Or at least he was trying. Knowing nothing of his temper or what was to come between us, I cooked for him that first morning out of love, not fear. It was the love of a new wife wanting to make her husband happy, to give him one more reason to brag to his friends about just how good "his woman" was.

I wanted to make him proud, but I didn't know the first thing about cooking grits. I stared at the sand-looking stuff I'd poured in the pot, and all I knew was that I had to make it rise. Not having a clue what to do and since it worked for cakes, I added baking powder and water. And I prayed, maybe too much. The grits rose clear across the stovetop, and all while I was screaming and chasing them back into the pot, Anderson stood in the doorway laughing.

"What the shit is this?" he asked, walking into the kitchen. I looked at him helplessly, and we both had a good laugh. We settled for bacon and loaf bread, and then it was back to bed.

The good Lord may not have saved my grits that morning, but Anderson and I had a story to tell for years to come.

It was five o'clock when we finally made it back to my parents' house. I was more comfortable by that time, but still anxious to see my family and get some clothes. My wedding gown was the only thing I had time to bring with me.

I didn't know what to expect when I got there. I knew my mama wouldn't approve of us disappearing like that, and moreover, that she'd known what we'd been doing.

"Your mama gon' say, 'Ain't no way my baby's been doing that'," Anderson joked. We laughed together because it was true. When the reverend asked me during the ceremony if I would forsake all others, my mama spoke up before I could get a word out.

"No, she won't forsake me," she said.

When we arrived, she scolded us for disappearing, and for not eating with the guests, but everyone was all smiles and laughter. I realized fully then that I no longer belonged to my parents. I was no longer their responsibility. From then on, I belonged to Bill Anderson.

He spent the next couple of days either in bed with me or in town, doing whatever. He never told me where he was going, or when he was coming back. I spent most of that time alone in his brother's house, daydreaming of our new life together, a new home in Oklahoma, our children, happiness.

He left on Friday morning, with promises to send for me in a few weeks. I didn't see him again for six months.

People ask me now if I saw warning signs there in the beginning, the control, the possessiveness. One can only know for sure in hindsight. At the time, I didn't know any better and the primary example of marriage I had was my mama and daddy who had a loving relationship.

I grew up during a time when battered women, in the physical and especially the emotional sense, did not exist. There were only troubled, pesky wives who didn't know how to properly take care of their husbands. Wives were property, similar to slaves, and as nosey and gossip-prone as people in my community were, the relationship between a husband and wife wasn't for meddling. Even when the wife walked around looking like she'd been hit by a bus.

I remember a woman named Minnie, who was the wife of a deacon in a local church while I was growing up. She was a small framed woman, about 4'11", and he was a giant who weighed about 250 pounds. He beat her almost every day, for being "lazy." He never lifted a finger to do anything himself. One of her chores was to milk the cows and walk the milk to the edge of the road for the milkman to pick up. He never went with her, but if he so much as thought that she'd missed the pickup, he'd beat her all the way back up the road. And she had nothing to say about it. Even if she wanted to leave, there was no place for her to go. She had no money, no ownership of anything for herself, no power.

Word about the abuse spread through the church and neighborhood like everything else, and as usual, I'd eavesdrop on every bit I could get from Ma Lil and my parents. When my daddy finally got nerve to ask the deacon why he beat on Minnie, he said that she deserved it for being so lazy. Said he even gave her a "break" on Saturday nights.

"I gotta get my soul right for church Sunday morning because I got to shout," he said. "And I make sure I don't touch her a full week before communion." Come Sunday afternoon, he'd be back on her again.

I thought about Minnie a lot while I was with Anderson. I understand that she was trapped in a way that I was not, because she had no education and no job of her own. She must've felt mixed relief and dread on Saturday nights, or during Communion week. How strong she must've been to keep her rage contained, to avoid doing something she might regret. When I thought of her, sadness crept in my spirit understanding that she probably never knew what love or romance was or possibly never felt anything at all.

But by the time Anderson left that Friday, I had no idea that we'd be connected in this way. None of us women looked for warning signs, and even if they were glaring, we would've ignored them for love and tradition.

If anyone did see something, it was my sister, Hattie. When Anderson left for Oklahoma, the first thing she did was pull me aside and tell me to get myself back in school.

"You never know what's gonna happen, Ella Mae," she said firmly. "You got to learn how to do for yourself, and don't be depending on no man to hold you up."

Unless something happened to Anderson in the military, I didn't believe that I'd ever be caught without my man to care for me. I only listened to Hattie because I trusted her words more than most, and I had dreams of my own.

Chapter 4

FORTUNATELY, or unfortunately, depending on how you looked at it, I knew several women whose husbands were in the army. Without the benefit of their experience, I may never have known the full extent of Anderson's lies about military life. But of course, sometimes, as they say, ignorance is bliss.

I learned by and by that despite what he told me, wives were welcomed to join their husbands in their travels around the country and abroad. I had a cousin who traveled the world while her husband was in the military. She had all her babies in different countries and decorated their home with art and furniture from everywhere they went. I wanted that kind of life for myself, wanted to see beyond Paw Creek and even New York, but Anderson never had those intentions for me. By December, I'd had enough and decided I couldn't sit and wait on him any longer.

I was living at home with my parents at the time, helping my mama around the house and rearing some of my nieces and nephews who were living there as well. Having already successfully made a living in a place like Harlem, I could no longer be satisfied making a meager living for myself in Paw Creek. I had no children of my own, no pressing responsibilities, nothing to keep me anchored to that small town. My cousin, Helen, had been trying to get me up to Connecticut for a while, just to see how I'd like it, and none of Anderson's letters were promising.

My Dearest Ella Mae,

Life on the base has not been what I expected. I'm searching for the perfect place where we can be together and raise our children. There ain't no place for you here that would feel like home with flowers and trees and cool breezes to relax your mind. I will continue searching and counting the days when we can be together again.

Love always, Bill

Christmas time was special because I knew Anderson would be home and I would be returning to Oklahoma with him to start our lives together. I packed my bags and placed them by the door in anticipation of his arrival. I ran onto the porch at the loud sound of his approaching vehicle. He leaped from the car grinning as if he delighted in seeing me as much as I did him. I ran to him, arms opened wide into his waiting embrace.

"How I missed you, Ella Mae," he said to me.

"I missed you too."

We kissed. He gripped my hand and led me to the car. "Let's go."

"Wait," I yelled as he pulled me toward the car. "I've got to get my stuff."

"You can get it when we come back. Right now, I want you to myself."

It was the happiest I had been in a long time. I chattered on about the things that had happened in our town until we arrived at his brother's house. My heart raced in anticipation of finally being with the man I loved. We were going to end the year with each other and start the new year afresh.

It was Christmas Eve, two days later when we returned to my parents' house. Mama was busy in the kitchen preparing the Christmas dinner. The smell of fresh baked pies and cakes met us outside. I couldn't wait to rush in so my mama could see how happy I was and how happy I had made Anderson when he realized I had learned to cook while he was away. His belly was full of the homemade biscuits and molasses I had made that morning. And the grits he ate were cooked perfectly without lumps and they stayed in the pot.

I rushed to the kitchen to help my mama prepare the greens while Anderson and my daddy sat in the front room. As usual, Anderson had a cigar sticking out the corner of his mouth and the loud laughter I heard let me know he and Daddy were getting along fine.

Mama and I had just finished the dishes and I was wiping my hands on an old rag when I heard Anderson talking.

"Life is hard out there in Oklahoma. Man can't hardly make it on a soldier's salary. I'm gonna leave Ella Mae here with you a few more months until I can save up for a nice place for the two of us."

I looked into the room and saw Daddy nod his understanding. When he saw me standing in the doorway, his eyes were sympathetic. I turned and walked away. It was then that I decided to see more of the world alone rather than not at all.

∞

Life in Connecticut was much like Paw Creek in many ways. It was a southern town placed up in the North. Everyone knew everybody, and even though it was racially mixed like New York, the lifestyle was the same—country. There's not much more to be said about it. I didn't like it very much.

I lived in a row house with my cousin, Helen and one other girl. I ended up working in a factory again, this time making mechanical parts. It wasn't as fun as jewelry smithing, but it was a job and I was happy to be supporting myself again. As always, I clung to the church for stability and for friendship. In the midst of so much uncertainty about my marriage, church was the only place that felt consistent, dependable. I was there six days out of seven, at choir rehearsal, at bible study, at Sunday school, for sermons and picnics, biding the time between Anderson's letters and phone calls. I was only nineteen, but I felt like an old wife, abandoned before her prime.

The thought of not getting the chance to be Anderson's wife depressed me at a level I never thought possible. Every letter or phone call with his excuses sank me deeper into a hole. I prayed. I pleaded. I did everything I could think of to be part of his new life, but it became clear that he didn't have a role for me. I ripped myself apart wondering what I'd done wrong, wondering why he expended so much effort for so long to marry me, but never once invited me to Fort Sill for so much as a visit. I'd never been prone to sadness or anxiety or despair or even self-consciousness. But all of this weighed so heavily on my heart that I stopped taking care of myself like I should. I broke down shortly after my twentieth birthday, and was rushed to the hospital. Helen sent for Anderson through the Red Cross right away.

"I had perfect attendance, and you're making me miss days for foolishness!" he shouted at me the moment he got through the door of the house. I'd been released by the time he got there, and in his opinion, I hadn't been in the hospital long enough for him to care.

"You're not sick enough for someone to have to come get me," he spat at me. "I've been sick plenty of times, and I've never needed you."

I hadn't seen his temper before, and it startled me a bit. But I was too drained and too happy to see him to argue, so I brushed it off as stress. Helen didn't.

"You don't need this," she ranted when we were alone. "Here you're the one laid up, and you're comforting him? Don't let him do this to you. I'll beat his ass."

I didn't listen. The only thing that mattered was him being there. It didn't matter that I had to convince him I had been sick, or that I spent the entire time trying to calm him down the only way I knew how, in the bed. All I needed to get back on my feet was him. I let it go. He left two days later, and he still didn't believe me. My cousin was the only one fuming.

When he finally did believe me, it was for the wrong reason.

∞

Ma Lil died the third week in September. She'd fallen and broken her leg a couple of weeks earlier and pneumonia came and took her away before any of us could make it down to say goodbye. She was in her nineties, and worked right up until she fell, still making her rounds to deliver babies around Paw Creek. I'd always thought that she'd be there to meet my babies when the time came.

Coming home was a blessing, despite the circumstances. I needed to be surrounded by all my family, to focus on being a daughter, a granddaughter and a sister, roles I knew far better than wife. I helped Mama with everything I could— the hosting, the cooking, the cleaning—whatever I could do to be useful and occupied.

The funeral was held at a small country church just outside of town. I don't remember much from the ceremonies except the way they had Ma Lil dressed. She looked like a little old church lady, all gussied up in a fancy dress and makeup. I realized then that I barely recognized her in those clothes because I can scarcely remember seeing her outside her midwife uniform. She didn't come around us often, but my aunt and cousin lived with her and always saw to it that her uniforms were washed, pressed, and hung for when she got home after her rounds.

If she had some time at home to relax, which was rare, you'd see her in her housecoat and slippers, something comfortable, but only for a little while. She stayed on the move, always in that grey dress, carrying that doctor's bag. She delivered white and black babies alike, because in those days, there were few doctors available and black women had always been the designated caretakers and nursemaids for southern babies, especially in rich white folks' houses. Ma Lil would always stay with the families for a while after the deliveries, just to make sure that the children were coming along alright, and to give the mothers a chance to recover. Then she'd be on her way, off to bring the next human into the world.

What stands out the clearest for me about Ma Lil was that she always had something to say to a girl or a young woman in the way of advice. Like my mama, she wanted to see us girls become more than just maids and housewives. She went so far as to open her home to teen girls who lived too far out in the country to attend the high school, just so they could get their diplomas. I felt her loss so deeply, in part, because I wish I'd known her better, wish she'd been able to slow down enough to spend more time being a grandmother. Giving life—her own for the sake of others—was her sacrifice for her community, and for us, though in our youth we couldn't see it.

The other thing I could never forget occurred when Mom hosted Ma Lil's wake at our house and all the family gathered there to eat and talk and reflect. My sister-in-law was sitting near me, and she was big and pregnant. She was a sight. I started joking with her about how big she'd gotten.

"Hush, Mae," she said, only half joking.

"Yes Mae, please hush, because you got no right to be laughing." Mama's cousin Junie was looking at me dead on with a funny kind of smile on her face. I looked back at her, confused. "You're pregnant too," she said, still smiling.

"What?" I laughed at her, but inside I was terrified. "Now Junie, I know you got to be crazy. I don't know nothing about being pregnant."

"It's true," she said, "but knowing about it and being it ain't exactly the same."

I didn't believe her, but the thought got to me just the same. I always wanted a big family, with lots of babies, but I hadn't even had a chance to be a good wife yet.

Nonetheless, a few weeks later, my period was late. Something new was growing inside me, and all I could do was pray and hope that we were ready. I felt like I needed Ma Lil then more than ever.

Anderson showed up for Ma Lil's visitation. He'd been assigned to pick up a soldier who had gone AWOL at Fort Jackson, which was only an hour away from Paw Creek. I saw none of his temper there because he was surrounded by my family, my sisters and brothers and aunts and cousins. He couldn't have gotten away with much, even if he'd wanted to.

I didn't mention any of what Junie said to me, not even as a joke. When it was time to tell him, I wrote him a letter that he received on base. I got a phone call back from him; I suspected it was because he was too excited to write.

"Don't be putting that on me," he said. "That's not mine."

"What?"

"You heard me. You got some nigger up there in Connecticut. I got it now. You couldn't handle it, so you called up the Red Cross so you could put it all on me."

I couldn't talk. I could barely even breathe. It was not possible that he believed this, not after writing to him every day, not after telling him how much I loved him. Not after pleading with him to let me come live with him. The pain surged through me and quickly turned to anger. I found my voice again.

"Anderson, how long does it take to make a baby?" My voice shook through the phone.

"I only saw you at Christmas and in Connecticut," he said back, raising his voice. "And you not gon' put that on me."

I felt myself getting smaller, the size of a beetle. The phone became heavy against my ear.

"If you believe I was with someone else, that's your business because I know the truth," I said to him finally. "The child will tell you who's the daddy anyhow."

∞

He wasn't there when Priscilla was born early the next year. I decided to stay in Paw Creek after Ma Lil died partly because my daddy insisted, and because I couldn't bear to go back to Connecticut. Helen had enough going on with her own family, and I'd been through too much there to return. I became a child again in a lot of ways, dependent once more on my parents to care for me because Anderson wouldn't. He never claimed Priscilla, not even after I sent him the pictures.

"I don't make girls," he wrote to me in a letter. In the end, he would make three. I laugh at the irony today, but at the time, it was devastating. I prayed for boys every time, hoping that for once, I could make him happy. A girl was always "some other nigger's child." I know now, though, that he would have found some way to put it on "some other nigger" even if I could have made that wish for a boy come true.

∞

First the shock, then the sting. I raised my hand to where his had been and quickly braced myself for the other that was coming down on me. It was December 1959, in my parents' house. Anderson told me he'd be home for the holidays, gave me an exact date. He showed up at the house a few days early from Fort Sill. I thought he wanted to surprise me, but in reality, he was trying to catch me with "my man."

His letters had changed. His suspicions were all he talked about in them and in the few phone calls we shared.

> *Ella Mae, I got the pictures you sent me of that baby. It don't look like me. I don't make girls. I better not ever catch you with that nigger. It will be bad for both of you.*
>
> *Bill*

I continued to send him pictures of Priscilla and told him everything about her. Somehow, I had made up my mind that if he continued to see pictures and how much she looked like him, he would accept her and things would return to how I had dreamt or better.

His only response was, "Yeah, I got the pictures. Better not be running around with no one." He'd call me sometimes twice a night not to see how I or the baby was doing but with accusations. "Better not have no man in bed with you." I decided it was pointless to try to convince him otherwise. The mere fact that we lived with my parents did not deter his suspicions. He'd invented the father of our child. He was going to believe whatever he wanted. I did hope, though, that he'd eventually see that it was all in his head. I never understood where the paranoia came from; if someone was filling his head with stories about me. I continued to press on, never letting his words affect me or my baby.

People say that men don't become fathers until they see their children in person. The next December was the first-time Anderson met Priscilla, and I believed that once he saw her, he couldn't deny her.

That was the first time he hit me.

"What I want with a girl?' he hissed at me in the bedroom. "That's just another baby. I wanted a boy. My daddy told me don't have no girls and I don't."

As cruel as he'd been, I never saw it coming. I don't remember much after that but shame. My body burned with it, and every muscle in my body tensed as I lay next to him for the rest of the night, tears pouring as he slept.

Anderson's father wasn't a violent man. He was mild-tempered and polite, and never tolerated any rowdiness from his boys. I expected the same from his son, but Anderson had other role models. His half-brother Paul was their mother's son from her first marriage. Paul grew up watching his father constantly beating on their mother before she remarried. Anderson and their other brother, Marcell, would have to pull Paul off his own wife when he began beating her several years later. I still can't imagine Anderson beating his own brother for beating his wife. I'll never know what made him do the same.

I told no one. I stuck to the stories I created in my head. It was a random incident. I overwhelmed him; he still hasn't gotten over not having a boy. He's afraid I'm cheating on him. He was just lashing out. Things will be better once we live together on base. Things will be better once we have a boy. Things will get better...

∞

In the summer of 1961, I was twenty-three years old and wanted to be a beautician. Priscilla was two by then, and New York was calling me back. Anderson was still stationed in Oklahoma. I'd only seen him twice since that Christmas. I was doing the same thing I was before Priscilla was born, helping my mama around the house, looking after my nieces and nephews. I had a job at one point, as the kitchen help in a "whites only" restaurant in town that was owned by the father of this white girl I knew when I was younger.

During my meal breaks, I had to eat in the back of the restaurant in the food storage pantry. My table was a crate of cabbages and my chair was a crate of canned goods. It was humiliating, but I dealt with it because it was good money. But one night, after we'd closed and cleaned up, I sat up on a bar stool in the front of the restaurant, just eating the last bite of my cornbread while I waited for them to let me out for the night. I was called into the manager's office two days later. When he told me that I couldn't be seen in the front of the store because "colored folks would see it and want to sit there too," I knew my time was up.

"What are you trying to start?" he said to me with his long southern drawl. He stood over me with glaring eyes. I thought any minute, he was going to hit me.

I left at the end of my shift, and never went back, not even for my paycheck. Here my husband was serving this country, and I couldn't show my black face at the front of a white-owned restaurant. I wasn't going to be his good nigger.

When my sister Hattie came to visit from Charleston, she told me it was time to move forward. She knew about Anderson's accusations and his refusal to let us move to Oklahoma so we could be a family. Somehow, she knew what it all meant long before I did. The control, the refusal to let me live with him, the denial of our child was all a prelude to what was going to happen. But, I was grown and she was going to let me live my own life and figure it out for myself.

"Go back to New York and do for you, Ella Mae," she told me. "Depend on you, and take care of that baby."

Anderson agreed to drive me to New York in June. He was going to be back in Paw Creek for his furlough then, and the trip would give us an opportunity to be alone together, away from work and home. I hoped we could finally work through some of our problems. I believed much of what was wrong had to do with things he wasn't telling me, things he was trying too hard to handle like a man and preserve his pride by not sharing with me. I had no idea what his work was like, but I could only imagine how stressful it could be. I saw him as any young army wife sees her husband, or rather, had to see him, in order to stomach the thought of him in battle: iron strong, stoic, and persevering. He just needed a break. We both did. And we would finally get one together.

∞

A few days before he got home, a letter came to my parents' house, an envelope addressed to Anderson from someplace else in town. I could've waited to give it to him when he got back, but I didn't. His secrecy about everything and my own eagerness to find out whatever I could trumped his privacy. *I am his wife*, I reasoned to myself. There should be no secrets between us. I opened the letter.

The letter was dated from a few days before. There was going to be a visit in New York. He would meet her after he dropped me off in Harlem. They would be together for a week before he drove back south. She loved him; she couldn't wait to see him. She was one of the girls he dated in school. From the looks of it, he'd never stopped. I was heartbroken but it only confirmed my suspicions. I got myself together and tucked the letter in a safe place.

We left Priscilla with my mama and started out to New York. He was quiet for most of the ride to Harlem, but that was nothing out of the ordinary. For once, I had nothing to say. I wasn't going to talk about it until we got to New York; I wanted to make sure he couldn't back out on another promise. The letter sat in my suitcase; my hands were set to rip it apart, but my head thought the better of it. He wouldn't be able to call me a liar this time. We'd been married a little over three years, and I couldn't remember a time when he wasn't accusing me of being unfaithful. My head swam.

When did he stop thinking of me as the girl who didn't mess around because her mama wouldn't let her out the house? Where was that girl in his head? Where was the woman he promised to always love? Maybe replacing me with a loose woman image made it easier on him when he went to be with her. Did he even need any justification?

I kept my face composed; I even found a way give an almost authentic smile when I needed to. It was my first time disguising that kind of rage. It was almost frightening how good I got at it. For one thousand miles, I sat there in his car, praying silently for my own peace, and hearing the voice of my sister in my head, "Depend on you, and take care of that baby." I knew that I had to do both now, and I'd made the right decision to do it, no matter what happened with him. Yes, I was still in love and no, it wasn't clear-sighted. Not at all. But at least I wasn't completely blind anymore.

As soon as I got settled into my place in Harlem, I pulled out the letter. He just stared at me. I looked for any sign of shock, surprise, or shame. I got none.

"What I do is none of your damn business," he said, pointing his finger in my face.

"Oh, but you seem to have a problem even thinking that I might be messing around." I pushed his hand away. "Calling me a liar all this time and look at you."

His fist cut me off. I snapped. I lunged at him with my full weight, and we tumbled to the floor. I kicked and scratched and bit and punched and shrieked as he caught my neck and slowed my breathing until I couldn't struggle anymore. My eyes widened as I focused all my energy on air. *Air.* Just as I felt myself fading, he slowly loosened his grip and leaned in close to my face.

"You ain't got shit to say about what I do," he barked at me. "I bought you, and you don't belong to nobody but me. You do what I want, when and where I want it. Don't let me have to tell you again." He slapped my face.

The sting of his assault was muffled by the tears that streamed down my face. I continued to struggle to catch my breath. His grip on my neck tightened every time I managed a gasp. I felt his other hand around my thigh, his thumb pressed hard into my skin as he forced himself between my legs. When he finally let go of my neck, I was too weak to fight, to resist him. He ripped my clothes off, first the stockings, then the blouse. He pushed my skirt up around my waist, unbuckled his pants.

"Please," I gasped. "Don't—" His hands went back around my neck, and he squeezed until I almost lost consciousness.

"Don't you say shit," he warned, releasing my neck and wrapping his palm around my mouth.

I closed my eyes and prayed once again for peace, as I felt his full weight moving against me. Tears streamed from my tightly closed eyes. Where was the young man I'd met so many years ago? Where was his smile, wit and charm? Where was the man I waited all my life to be with? He wasn't here. I wondered what the army had done to make him such a cruel, vicious being. He left as a young man full of hope and returned an animal mean enough to kill. I didn't want him to touch me, but he was there violating me against my will. When he was finished, he stood over me, dressing and daring me to say anything. He left for several hours and returned later that night and acted as if nothing had happened.

∞

I worked full-time at a battery factory this time. The men would work in the lifting and shipping department, and women were stationed at the assembly lines. It was tedious, but it paid well. I was in good company, and I made some friends there over time. In the evening I took night classes at Poro Beauty College over on 116th Street, working mostly on hair styling. My goal was to work as an instructor at a beauty college somewhere, maybe in New York or maybe back home. Anderson sent me money every month, but it wasn't much, and I wanted to make sure that Priscilla would never have to go without anything.

Despite the circumstances, it was good to be back in Harlem. It was the only place that felt like mine. Life hadn't changed much in my neighborhood since I'd left, but the country felt like it was moving in a new direction. Southern blacks were starting to demand their rights in boycotts and protests; the murder of a young black boy from Chicago while visiting his uncle in Mississippi had gotten worldwide press. Martin Luther King, Jr was a living man whose name was new on our lips. Seemed like for the first time in my life, people were finally showing the rage I felt the day I threatened that white couple. I hoped that my mom would live to see the day when she wouldn't get paid white people's leftovers for a full day's work.

Most importantly for me at the time was my own freedom. Funny how quickly your enemies can change faces and colors. I think that given another life, I might've joined the black freedom movement and fought for first-class citizenship. Instead, I fought against my own husband for basic respect and dignity. The only thing that mattered then was that I was winning, even if it was the small triumph of being strong enough to get back out into the world.

I still wrote to him almost every day, hoping that he'd open up and we could put everything behind us. I forgave him and I wanted us to move forward. It was most of what I prayed for at church, before bed, at meals, on the subway and on the assembly line. His letters didn't change. Each one was just a different version of the one that had come before: *"Betta not be messin' with them niggers."*

The church continued to be my sanity. I couldn't go as much as I did before because of my night classes, but I was there every weekend. I returned to Canaan Baptist in Harlem and found most of my old friends still there. One of them,

Rita, became my roommate. She was an Alabama native, sweet and street savvy. And she saved my life.

I woke up one Sunday morning in February 1961 soaked in blood. The pain nearly took my breath away. I hadn't seen my period in two months. I crawled out of bed, and hobbled as fast as I could to Rita's room.

"Call the ambulance," I gasped, and fell to my knees. She and her boyfriend had just woken up. She screamed when she saw the blood. Within minutes, she'd wrapped me up as best she could and had her boyfriend call an ambulance. I was still on her bedroom floor. She looked at me, her eyes wide and watery.

"You think you're pregnant?" she asked.

It would've been a boy.

Chapter 5

I MOVED TO FORT SILL, Oklahoma in April 1962.

I don't know what made Anderson change his mind about living together, but I do remember feeling like it would be a new beginning for us. It had been less than six months since the miscarriage. He didn't deny it was his, but perhaps it would've been better for me if he did. He beat me senseless.

"Why did you keep that other nigger's baby and let mine die?" he asked me in a letter.

The doctor never mentioned the cause of death, but I still believe it was stress. My body was too busy recovering from my husband to take care of his son. But there was no telling him that.

Everything had to be put on hold. My career as a beautician, my clients, and a shop of my own all had to wait for him. I was a few weeks away from graduating from Poro and had been looking forward to graduating on a stage with my family watching and cheering, but when Anderson said, "Now," there was no negotiation. They mailed my license to Oklahoma.

Priscilla was there too. She had just turned three years old, and she called me "Ella Mae," just like Mama did. I wasn't bothered by that; Mama had been her mama from the beginning. I was just happy that I was finally getting the chance to settle down in a house with her and my husband, my family. I can remember thinking that this was what we needed all along—what Anderson needed. He needed to be like the other married men on the base, coming home to a family that was his, a home-cooked meal, and some loving at nighttime. It was simple enough, and I knew that I could do it, that I wanted to do it, every day. We could put the past five years behind us and he would never need to seek another woman's touch again.

Oklahoma was hot and dry. It was as far west as I'd ever been and it looked in some parts like some place out of a John Wayne movie, with the flat land and the tumbleweeds. Our house was in the suburb of Fort Sill, away from the main strip and the military base, which Anderson declared was out of bounds for me.

"Women don't need to be on the base with all of those men," Anderson would say. "A man who lets his wife live and shop on the base doesn't think much of her."

The people were friendly. Many of the women in the area were army wives like me and had come from all over the country to raise their families in that little tumbleweed town. By and by I got to know quite a few of them. I met most of them over at the neighborhood dumpster and seeing that I was the new girl on the block, they'd come over to visit and make me feel welcome.

It was funny how the military didn't seem to know what was happening in the rest of the country. It was 1961 and you would have thought that Martin Luther King's beloved community had sprouted in my back yard. There was no segregation. Black soldiers had white wives and lived next door to white families. White army wives dropped by my house to visit me and Priscilla, and Anderson trained alongside soldiers of all colors and eventually fought beside men who he would have had to call "sir" if he came across them in the South. The irony of a small Oklahoma town feeling even more integrated than New York City was strange, but it made me hopeful that the country could someday get past the color line.

I had a girlfriend, Sadie, who lived next door and would always come over to visit Priscilla and me while Anderson and her husband were in training. Clearly, her husband didn't see things the way Anderson did. Sadie did as she pleased—there was nowhere she couldn't go and she wouldn't hear of being policed by any man. When I told her about Anderson's boundaries, she looked at me like she smelled something rotting in my kitchen.

"But you don't listen to him, right?" she asked, as if there was only one acceptable answer. "I mean, you are a grown woman. You're not some lap dog he can command."

"Well, but—"

"But what, Ella Mae?" She stared at me, shaking her head. "Do you tell him where to go and what to do when he gets there? Now are you gonna come with me to the base, or are you gonna stay here and be a chicken?"

Somebody saw us. Sadie, Priscilla and I had gone out shopping on the base—at the PX and the commissary—and I suppose I enjoyed it so much that I forgot to be discreet. The PX was its own world and, more importantly, it was Anderson's world. This was the place that he hated to leave for any reason, the place that made him proud of who he was, something that a wife and a child had not yet been able to do for him. It wasn't glamorous or chic like the malls where you got all dressed up to shop, but I liked it better than the stores Anderson made me go to downtown because it was more convenient and because I liked feeling that I was part of his world, even if it wasn't what he wanted.

The bruises he left on my face couldn't be concealed. He'd ask about me around the base, checking to see if I was following his orders. The soldiers and the storekeepers kept watch over my comings and goings for him. And when they didn't, his imagination, though often far off the mark, did it for him. And what had previously been two random episodes of abuse in our distant marriage became a daily ritual, almost as ordinary as doing chores or brushing my teeth. I was terrified, but Sadie was angry. She hated my husband.

"Girl you better fight back. *Fight back!*" She looked at my face in horror. "I ain't gon' have no man beating me like that, and you better not either."

Anderson never hit me in front of other people, not even Priscilla. He was careful that way. But all anybody had to do was look at me to know what was going on.

Still, he was charming to most people. Even if people didn't approve of what he did at home, it was still the early '60s and a battered woman didn't mean what it means now.

"I bought you," he told me again one night after a particularly bad beating. "Anytime you buy something, it becomes your property and you use it however you want to. I don't have to give you a reason."

He drank heavily almost every day. He'd stumble in the house at the end of the day and the fights seemed to start as soon as he shut the door. The house wasn't clean enough. I didn't make the meal he wanted. Priscilla would be crying too much. He used any excuse to ram his fist into my face or my stomach, or my head. I never touched him except for when I was trying to block the force of his blows. Touching him in any way, however gentle, was just another reason for him to beat me. The closest we got to one another was when he raped me and that was just another means to enforce his rules.

I found out I was pregnant again in June of 1962. The beatings didn't stop.

The closest he ever came to hitting me in front of his friends was a Sunday evening in July of the same year. Everyone knew that I was barely let out of the house, so

Anderson's friend, Thomas came over with his wife, Anita and Sadie brought her husband, James for one of my home-cooked dinners. It was a feast. There was chicken, potatoes, black-eyed peas, rice, greens and cornbread. Everybody had seconds and Anderson talked through the meal like everything was right with the world, even as I sat beside him with a bruised eye.

"That was a great meal, Ella Mae," James said to me, smiling. "Anderson, you're a lucky man to get cooking like this every night."

Anderson looked over at me and looked quickly back at his plate. "A man will eat shit if he's hungry," he mumbled.

Sadie's jaw dropped slightly, and the table got quiet. I felt the heat rise in my cheeks and I stood up and started clearing the dishes off the table.

"Let's go out for dessert," Sadie suggested. "We can just walk over to the ice cream parlor. It's nice out and it'll be good to get some fresh air."

Anderson didn't object.

Sadie, Anita and I walked together with Priscilla to the ice cream parlor while the men went ahead of us, talking. Priscilla was the only one of us smiling. She loved ice cream and she was so happy to get out of the house.

"You ok, Ella Mae?" Anita asked. I wasn't sure how to answer that. Even though I had been insulted, the day was better than most because we had company and I knew that he wouldn't dare touch me. But I was miserable. There was never any peace, and I was terrified of what would happen to Priscilla, the new baby, and me. We were completely dependent on Anderson for everything—shelter, clothing, food—something that I'd worked so hard to avoid. I couldn't work out there, and I never saw any of his money. There were times when there wasn't enough food for us. I'd plead with him. I wasn't so much worried about me, but I couldn't let anything happen to Priscilla or the baby. I would fight for them.

"That's your kid," he'd say. "You better figure out how to feed her yourself because I'm not giving you anything. I eat on the base."

We lived from minute to minute, one day at a time. And at that minute, things were as good as they were going to get.

"I'm fine," I said finally.

When we got to the ice cream parlor, Anderson had already ordered butter pecan for himself. I asked him to get some chocolate for Priscilla because it was her favorite, but he refused.

"I already got what I want and that's all I'm paying for," he said. "She's your kid. You get it for her." He knew I didn't have any money, and I didn't dare ask any of the others to get it for her, because that was a sure beating. He didn't want anyone thinking that he couldn't provide for his family, even if he didn't claim us.

Pricilla cried all the way back to the house, and the more she cried, the angrier I got. We sat back at the table, and I tried to get her to calm down, but she wouldn't. He just sat there, eating his ice cream right in front of her like she was invisible. I snapped.

"If she's not gonna have her ice cream, nobody is." I got up, grabbed everyone's ice cream and washed all of it down the sink. Anderson gave me a look that I knew meant trouble. I didn't care.

"You must've lost your mind," he said, standing up from the table.

"Yeah, I must've lost the rest you didn't already beat out of me," I replied, staring him down.

"I think we should go," James said. He, Sadie, Thomas and Anita got up from the table. Sadie grabbed Priscilla.

"We'll take her out for some ice cream, ok, Ella Mae?" They all filed out the back door and Anderson shut it behind them. He came right at me and I was ready. I shielded my stomach as best I could from his fists and fought back as hard as I could. We brawled from the kitchen, to the living room, to the bedroom for at least twenty minutes. He slammed my head against the wall and I slapped him across his face. He tried kicking me in the stomach, but I caught his leg and pulled as hard as I could until he fell to the ground. I crawled away and he grabbed at me. I scratched and bit and punched as much as I could, and he kept the blows coming. By the time Sadie got back with Priscilla, who had had an extra scoop of chocolate and was smiling from ear-to-ear, I wasn't the only one with bruises. And that was what mattered most to me.

To their credit, people tried to help. The landlord confronted him and said, "You're not supposed to be hitting no woman." Sadie tried to get me to go with her to turn him in to his company commander, but I wouldn't. I couldn't.

"You don't have to go around here looking like that, Ella Mae," she said, pleading with me. "Don't be chicken about this."

I couldn't risk it.

"Don't you know they would take my rank from me?" he said to me one night, drunk. "You're not gonna do that. That'd be a good reason to kill you."

I weighed the decision. No one would be able to get to me fast enough and I couldn't even think about what he might do to Priscilla if I couldn't protect her. I said nothing. And the abuse continued until he sent me home to have my baby in December.

Eight months. That was the longest stretch of time I ever got to live with him in Oklahoma. As Christmas approached, Anderson decided that he couldn't stand the sight of me anymore. The baby was three months away, and he wasn't going to take any time from his work to take me to the hospital.

"You're getting on my nerves," he said. "You need to go home to your mama, where somebody loves you." I didn't fight him on that. To my knowledge, the baby was still healthy, but I knew that another three months of beatings and blows to my stomach would be pushing far past my luck.

It's difficult to explain how I felt about him then. Any dreams I had about a normal, happy family were destroyed by each fist that came down on my head or my chest. Each kick in the stomach reminded me that with him, there was no such thing as love. It existed only in my dreams, and now I was fully awake. But awake didn't mean free. It meant only that I was aware for the first time that I had married into my worst nightmare. And with divorce being almost unheard of, especially for black folks in the sixties, it meant that I was trapped.

I couldn't hate him. I think that's the one thing the women of my generation had to learn. When divorce isn't an option, hate is also not an option, because if you allow it in, one of you will end up dead, the other probably behind bars. I also couldn't hate him for my children's sake, not only because it would ruin them, but also because in a way, hating him would mean hating them. He was just as much a part of them as I, even if he never admitted it, and I would give my life for them. I suppose the best way to describe how I felt about him was obligated. Not out of any kind of romantic love, but because of our contract before God and my commitment to our children. Because of that, for the next eighteen years, I focused all my energy on being the best mother I could be and staying alive so that I could continue in that role.

∞

Lisa was a survivor. Of all my children, she suffered the most, starting in the womb. By the time Anderson, Priscilla and I began the long ride from Oklahoma to Paw Creek in December, I was amazed that she was still alive. I'd blocked as many blows as I could, but he went after her every time. Part of me still prayed that it was a boy, for the child's sake more than mine. I thought that maybe if Anderson finally got a son, he wouldn't ignore him the way he did Priscilla. And maybe he'd quit drinking so much and we could start being somewhat normal. Maybe I could see him happy, just once. Maybe I was just fooling myself.

The snow was thick on the roads and in the air. We could hardly see anything, but Anderson was determined to get me home and get himself back to Fort Sill before anybody could miss him. He only stopped to get gas on road trips, so if we had to use the restroom or if we were hungry, it had to wait until he needed the same things. When he did stop, there was a time limit. "If you're not back in the car in five minutes, you can find your own way home," he always said. I adapted. I got extra food for me and Priscilla whenever we stopped, and made sure she went to the bathroom every time, even if just to try.

The searing pain made its presence known somewhere in Georgia. It started in my lower stomach and crept up my back. I held my breath. *Cramps*, I told myself. Nothing I couldn't handle. I leaned back in the seat and focused straight ahead. The road was empty; it seemed like we were the only people in the world. It was pitch black outside and freezing, and the roads were still thick with snow, though it had finally stopped falling. All I could see ahead of me were sheets of fresh snow glowing in the headlights just before the crunching plow of our tires. Watching it was hypnotic. The pain soon dulled and I closed my eyes waiting for it to pass.

It didn't. I don't know how much time passed or how many miles, but the slow cramps turned to swift stabs, sharp, breath stealing, and all too familiar. The agony ushered my mind to a place where I witnessed it all over again, the blood-soaked sheets, the terror on Rita's face, the hospital bed, and the doctor's news.

Not this time.

We'd been through too much and she was too close to making her appearance in my world, too close to my arms to let her go.

Not this time.

"Stop the car." I braced myself against the door handle.

"You outta your mind."

"It's the baby," I choked. I bent over in the seat, tears dripping onto my coat. I could hear Priscilla stirring in the back seat, waking up.

"Something's wrong with the baby." I managed to look up at him when I said it.

He looked right back at me. His lips spread into a sinister grin, like the school bully cornering his next victim.

"That's *your* problem," he said sharply.

I flushed hot. The muscles in my back and neck tensed against my spine; I couldn't keep my hands from trembling. The pain was still there, but it felt almost faint compared to another familiar feeling taking over my body. I hadn't felt it that powerfully since the day I confronted the white couple and their baby. The muscles in my jaw pushed through my cheeks as my teeth clenched and grinded. If I touched him, neither the baby nor I would survive the night. But if he kept driving, I was sure I'd lose her.

Not this time.

We passed a large embankment on the highway. From the passenger window, I saw a sign for a motel at the top of the hill. The vacancy sign was lit. It was the first sign of life I'd seen in miles. By that point, the pain gripped my stomach so tightly, I could barely breathe. I wrapped my arm around my midsection and quickly looked back at Priscilla. Her head nodded as she fought to drift back to sleep. The vacancy light glared down at me from the hill.

"Pull over."

"I told you—"

"Now!"

He laughed softly under his breath and said, "You asking for it."

I knew what that meant. There was a stoplight ahead. He started to slow the car and I clenched the handle. As soon as he stopped, I opened the door and pushed myself onto the road, still holding my stomach as tightly as I could. I fell onto my side and slid a little, the dirty snow quickly soaking through my ripped stockings and underwear. When I looked up, I saw Anderson's arm reaching out for the door handle, pulling it shut while Priscilla cried in the back seat. The tires screeched and they were gone.

Something in me snapped then, like an overstretched rubber band. The highway turned into a blurry mix of gray and black. I looked around me. Nothing. No traffic. No people. No sound except the wind sweeping wisps of sparkling snow off the embankment and up the empty highway.

If we were at home on a night like this, the silence would've been comforting. Priscilla would be asleep in her room after I read to her and gave her some hot chocolate or milk. Anderson would be drunk or passed out somewhere where he couldn't touch me. And I'd be in the kitchen or bundled on the porch, watching the snowdrifts, thinking about those rare snow days when we were all young, and I still believed he was part of a fairy tale. But this silence made me feel dead, more so than at the end of all the beatings, all the screaming fights. I knew that if I didn't move soon, there'd be no chance to feel alive again.

I looked again for the vacancy sign, and found it at the top of the embankment just behind me. I was still lying on my side, and my arm was still clinging to my stomach. I pushed myself up onto my knees and rested there for a few minutes, my bare hands sinking into the gray slush. The stabbing pains were still in my stomach, but the cold was distracting. My arms and legs were numb, my movements stiff and awkward as I crawled toward the embankment. It was long, but not too steep.

The further I crawled, the less I could feel my body. The wind picked up, or at least it felt that way, and my face stung where the tears had frozen. I prayed with every step I took. The snow was a few inches deep and I couldn't see even the outline of my hands or feet. I pictured myself falling into a hole in the hill or losing my footing and sliding back onto the highway. Every solid piece of ground, every rock I found was miraculous. I prayed and I clawed; God only knows for how long. When I finally hobbled through the door of the motel, the desk clerk's face told me everything I needed to know. I looked like hell walking.

"I need a doctor." I fell to my knees and held my stomach with both arms.

"What the hell?" The desk clerk rushed to my side. "Ma'am, where did you come from? What happened?"

"Never mind that," I said. "Just get me a doctor, please."

"She's all right."

Everything that had begun to thaw froze up again. He'd followed me. I looked behind me and there he was with Priscilla wide-eyed and scared in his arms, looking down at me with the same grin he had in the car.

"Sir—"

"I said she's fine. She don't need a doctor. She's my wife. We just came here to rest for the night is all."

The desk clerk looked back down at me doubtfully.

"You're sure?" the clerk asked me. I couldn't speak. I couldn't risk it.

"We'll take a single room," Anderson said. He grabbed my arm, tightly, but not too forcefully and lifted me to my feet. He put Priscilla down and she clung to my other arm so tightly the beds of her little fingernails turned white.

"It's okay, baby," I whispered to her. "We're gonna go to bed now."

I still felt the pain, but not as sharp. I kept one arm around my stomach, and one around Priscilla as we walked to the room. The clerk watched me until we were out of his sight. I knew he wanted to help, but I'd taken too many risks for one night. I prayed with every step toward the room.

"Lord, keep us."

"Lord, keep us."

I must've said it fifty times by the time we got to the door. Priscilla and I shuffled inside as quickly as we could and she ran to the bathroom.

"I oughta kill you tonight." He said it in my ear, holding me to him by the arm I'd wrapped around my stomach. But he knew better. He didn't touch me again that night. And I didn't sleep. I held Priscilla tight to me, her head against my stomach and I prayed over and over again, "Lord, keep us. Lord, keep us."

Chapter 6

WE FINALLY REACHED Paw Creek the next day, I clung to my mama like Priscilla had clung to me in the motel lobby. "Well now, Anderson, y'all must got it pretty bad out there, 'cause I never seen Ella Mae this happy to be home." Mama wore her flowered house dress and had her white hair twisted in tight curls. She looked like an angel to me and her home like heaven.

I didn't look at him when she said it, but I felt his eyes on me. I heard the grin in his voice.

"Well I told her wasn't nothing out there but dust and tumbleweed." He laughed. "But you know, Ella Mae. She had to see for herself. Ain't no place for a woman."

I watched him drive away from my parents' house in his white '55 Impala and waited until it disappeared around the corner.

My mama saw me out on the porch, and came and wrapped her arms around me. "He'll be back, Ella Mae."

My teeth clenched. She didn't know any better. I grabbed her hand and gave her a little smile. "I know it."

∞

The next two months were quiet. I was a daughter again, doing chores around the house, running errands and cooking. Priscilla smiled more and slept better. Lisa was quiet, too; sometimes too quiet for my comfort. My hand stayed on my belly. She'd kick every once in a while, and I'd breathe a little easier, but as soon as it was over, I'd start waiting for the next one, sometimes for a couple of days.

"Chile, the baby's not supposed to be tap dancing." Mama saw me put my hand on my stomach for the ump-teenth time. "Leave it alone."

"Priscilla moved more."

"No two babies the same. Leave it alone."

I barely remember Christmas that year. Anderson came and went in a day and didn't touch me, but Priscilla and I were still on edge. She'd normally talk your head off, but around him, she kept to herself.

"You don't wanna say hi to your daddy?" Priscilla peeked out from behind Mama when Anderson came to the door. She gave him a little wave, and buried her head back into Mama's leg.

He waved back and laughed. "She don't take too easily to men," he said. "That's good. Won't have to be running boys off with my shotgun later on."

Everyone laughed but me. I stayed in the house instead of seeing him off when he left the next day.

Daddy came up to me one day after Christmas while I was folding laundry in my room. He'd just gotten back from church and he was watching me from the doorway. I didn't notice.

"What's wrong with you, girl?"

I jumped. My hands went straight to my stomach and chest.

"I scare you? I'm sorry, honey." He came over and sat down next to me. My dad was tall and skinny, towered over me even as we sat.

"Nothing's wrong." I kept folding. "How's everything at church?"

"Fine, fine. Everybody's asking 'bout you, happy to see you home. But you walking 'round here looking miserable."

I thought about it. Telling him I knew how Minnie felt every time she missed the milkman and the thoughts that must've gone through her head while she watched her husband play deacon to an admiring congregation. I wanted so much for him to know what it was like to dread the sound of his footsteps leading up to our front door in Oklahoma and how wide Priscilla's eyes got when she knew he was coming, like the boogieman was after her. How it felt to know that Anderson didn't claim Priscilla and how I worried that she'd grow up thinking something was wrong with her because her daddy didn't love her. I could feel my heart beat in my throat.

"I'm alright, Daddy." I stopped folding and turned to him. "I'm just tired. Ready for the baby to get here."

He looked at me for a minute, searching for a hint. He wasn't convinced, but he left it alone. He got up, rubbed my shoulder, and headed out of the room.

"Just a few more weeks, Ella Mae."

I didn't lie. Other than worrying about the baby and losing sleep because I was afraid I'd miss a kick; I was much better. If Daddy had seen me in Oklahoma, he'd've understood why he scared me in the doorway. I hadn't allowed myself to be caught off guard in months.

The first-time Anderson caught me not paying attention, he wrapped his arm around my neck and squeezed so tightly, I thought I would faint.

"Uh, huh," he whispered in my ear. "Thought your nigger had ya, didn't you?"

Well if he did have me, I'd hope he wouldn't treat me like that. I kept my guard up from that day on.

∞

She came early, but she was healthy. I was almost terrified to look at her when the doctor handed her to me, but when I finally did, I searched all over for marks, defects, any signs of what he'd done. She was perfect. I never told anyone at home what we'd been through for eight months and no one knew about the night on the highway except me, Anderson, Priscilla, and the motel clerk. Lisa was born in February and once again, I wrote a letter to Anderson telling him that he had a daughter. Once again, he denied she was his.

"I told you I don't make girls," he wrote. "You not gon' put her on me either."

My dad took Anderson's place at the hospital, as he did the first time, pacing the halls and twisting his favorite hat in knots. When she finally arrived and I'd finished my inspection, he came up to me, his forehead still creased.

"Ella Mae, you got to stop having these babies." His hat was balled up in his hand. "You know I can't take this stuff."

"Daddy, what you talkin' about? You and Mama did this eight times." We looked at each other for a couple of seconds and burst out laughing. The creases relaxed, but you could still see the lines in his forehead. He swatted me on the arm with his hat.

"Hush. That was different. I was younger, and that was your mama."

"Well, I'm the mama now."

"You still my little girl."

When we came home, Mama was waiting in the kitchen with a bucket of dirty dishwater to bathe Lisa, like she'd done with Priscilla, and all of the grandchildren for the first week of their lives. She said it made our arms and legs strong. Whether it was true or not didn't matter. All that did matter to me was that she was alive, and healthy.

I slept. Lisa was a quiet baby and Mama was all too happy to watch over her new grandbaby. I'd forgotten how it felt to relax, to let my body sink into the bed and to stop thinking, stop worrying. My dreams had been nothing but terror— blood, bruises, black eyes, babies dead by his hand or in my womb. I lived every moment, sleep or awake, in anticipation of the next fight, the next look in the mirror to see what else I needed to conceal. I'd never seen a war front, but I felt like he'd given me enough practice to be battle ready. What I didn't learn was how to recover from the aftermath.

Mornings were the hardest. Getting out of bed hurt; my entire body ached as the tension let go of my muscles a little more every day. I thought of it like thawing from a deep freezer; I had to relearn how to breathe normally, to talk and move and act without restraint. I had to learn how to live again. Priscilla did too, though thankfully, she recovered faster than I did. She focused all her energy on two things: playing and looking after her little sister.

I started smiling again.

"You looking better," Daddy said to me one day.

I was in the kitchen with Lisa, singing to her. "This little light of mine, I'm gonna let it shine..."

Priscilla was singing along, and bouncing around the stove.

"Yeah, Daddy. Much better." The relief on his face was comforting. I decided then that I wouldn't say anything to him about Anderson unless I had no choice.

That year was a quiet year for me, but not for my country. America was obsessed with nuclear weapons, communism, and black freedom. President Kennedy reaffirmed the nation's superpower status by solving the Cuban Missile Crisis; students were staging sit-ins against racial segregation across the country and James Meredith became the first black student at Ole Miss. Paw Creek, like the rest of the South, was still struggling with school integration and everybody had something to say about it.

"We deserve better than what we getting. If they wanna put us in there with the white kids, then the better for us," some of the teenagers would say.

"All we need is the money. Nobody said anything about needing to go to their schools. We got our own..." This was the cry of others.

"Them honkies don't want us there and I'm not about to put my kids somewhere they're not wanted," parents complained.

I hadn't given much thought to where I wanted my kids to go to school, but I did know that I didn't want them growing up feeling inferior to anyone. And I wanted them to go much further than I'd gotten in almost twenty-five years. But much more than all of that, I wanted them never to go through what I was going through with Anderson. No one wants that for their children, but the fear of it took over my thoughts and changed how I raised them. They were what was good about my marriage and if I couldn't protect them, my relationship and in some ways my life, would feel worthless. I stayed on my knees, nights and mornings, praying that they would never dread their husbands' footsteps or touch. I prayed they would never have to use makeup to hide abuse and they would never have to put one of their children at risk to save another as I did with Priscilla that night on the highway. I still pray for those things today.

I got back to basics. My sister, Hattie's words meant more to me now than ever. I had to have my own money to survive Anderson. He still sent checks every month, but they were barely enough to feed two mouths, let alone three. But Mama still needed me around the house and I had to stay home to look after Priscilla and Lisa.

One Easter, Hattie told me I should start charging her for doing her hair. It was at that moment I decided to finally put my Poro license to use.

"You got a gift, Ella Mae," she said, looking in the mirror. "It's time for you to be getting something for it."

I let her slide for free, as always, but I charged everyone else. Word got around town that I was good, and trained in New York, and soon I had a group of regulars. Once I got going steady, I got a job working as an assistant at a beauty school in town. Some of what I made went to church and my parents, but most of it went to savings, our survival fund. Priscilla would watch me pressing somebody's hair in the kitchen or giving her an up-do, and she'd go trying to do the same thing to her hair.

"Mama, look!" She'd come prancing into the kitchen with her hair standing straight up on her head, grinning so big.

We all got a good laugh, even Mama.

"What we gonna do with you, Prissy?" Mama would shake her head, still giggling. "That little girl's got nerve for days."

I still wrote to Anderson, but less often. I'd tell him how the girls were doing, how fast they were growing and how much I wished he were a bigger part of their lives. All of it was true, though I never expected it to happen. I just wanted to make sure he knew that the door was always open for him to be their daddy, no matter what happened with us.

"Don't know what you telling me about them for," he'd write back. "They not mine. Better not be with no nigga."

I told him that I did some hair from time to time, but I never said a word about the money. Watching it grow every week gave me more power than I'd felt since the first time I moved to Harlem. No one was going to take that away from me, from us.

Since I got married, I hadn't learned much about romance and nothing of sex and foreplay—what all the songs called making love. But what I had learned was how to survive, how to fight. Of all the things my mama had instilled—and sometimes beaten—into me, being a soldier wasn't one of them. Not that I blamed her. She'd never had to fight my daddy. I did remember, though, how worried she'd been about my getting married young and uneducated, how much she'd preached to us about being independent and learned, rather than focusing on supporting a man. It was all well intentioned and true, but in the end, in her eyes, my marriage trumped everything she said, just as her own took priority over anything she may have wanted for herself. If there was something, and there always is, she never said it out loud. I thanked God every day that I'd at least gotten to pursue one thing for myself. Even though it wasn't everything, it was progress. I think Ma Lil would've been proud.

For the next three years, we saw Anderson only three times, all during Christmas, and all while we were either living in or near my parents' house. He put on his usual charm, making jokes with my daddy, complimenting my mama's cooking. He even held Lisa and let Priscilla sit on his lap. We never touched. That was just fine with me.

"You can tell them about what I did, but no one will ever believe you," he said to me one night. "I've got two personalities."

That was the truest statement he'd ever made in our entire marriage.

From time to time, Mama would ask about why I didn't just take the girls and go back to Oklahoma.

"Was it that bad, baby? I bet you could have lots of clients out there. And what about the girls? They need to grow up with their daddy, don't you think?"

I always dreaded those conversations. More than my shame about the abuse, I was embarrassed that I had allowed this to happen. So much of my thinking at that time was about blame, where to place it. I did blame him, but it was mostly for fooling everyone into believing that he was decent, even caring. The rest I placed on me, for everything from stupid fights to losing his son. How could I tell her that I had become a human punching bag? That my marriage was just a big charade for our family? I couldn't bear the disappointment, the blame. I already felt more guilt than I could handle.

"Well, you heard what he said, Mama," I'd say. "I pushed him so hard about going up there and it just wasn't for me. That's his world."

She always gave me the same look, eyebrows raised, suspicious.

"I'll see about getting him to visit more often, Mama. But you know how it is."

"I know that you got two little girls growing up without their daddy. I don't see how y'all are any different from other families living on the base."

"You're right." I'd always give in. "We'll try it again."

It took five more years to make good on that promise.

In the meantime, Anderson bought the house across the street from my parents' home, a small white house with a front and back yard, and a small front porch. He just took the girls and me over to the house one day and handed me the keys. I hated it. I'd always dreamed of a home with giant windows where the sun could completely fill the house, brightening all the colors I put inside. Everything in this house, from the white frame to the small windows, made everything inside seem dim.

"I ain't no henpecked man," he said when I confronted him about it. "It's my money, my house. You don't have anything to say about it."

I consented and went about trying to make the house a home for my children. I didn't have a choice. Bright yellow kitchen walls with matching gingham curtains covered the windows above the sink. The girls' room was painted pink with matching bedspreads I got from the general store in town. The paneled living room held a sofa with bold colored pillows and a fireplace for those cold winter nights. It was a home when he was gone and hell when he came back.

It was bold of him, buying a house right near my parents. Almost like a challenge to see how long he could beat their daughter in front of them before they had anything to say about it.

I did miss Oklahoma, but of course, he had nothing to do with it. I missed Sadie and Anita, and the rest of the families on our block. I missed spending my days shopping in town or sipping on sweet tea while I watched Priscilla play from our porch on long summer days. If not for him, I would've been happy to raise our children there, where they could play with children of all colors, far away from the southern trap.

When he called on me to visit him in the summer of 1965, all I could think of was seeing my friends again. Sadie and I kept in touch by letter. I wrote her more than Anderson by that point. We made plans to have dinner and catch up, though admittedly, with Anderson gone, there wasn't much to tell from my end.

My girls were growing. Prissy was learning to read, and Lisa was walking and talking as best she could, but she was a shy one. Mama and Daddy were getting old, but they were making it. Daddy's church continued to grow and he provided more for Mama, which made him very proud and made Mama too proud to wash white people's laundry for table scraps anymore. She worked less, and spent more time laughing and singing and spoiling her grandbabies.

∞

Meanwhile, the world, it seemed, was crazier than ever. We lost our president in November of 1963, just as I was putting the finishing touches on a neighbor's hair. Martin Luther King spoke in front of thousands of restless black and white folks about racial unity in Washington, DC. Medgar Evers was shot in the back of the head in front of his own house for fighting Jim Crow. Fannie Lou Hamer, a sharecropper with a middle school education, started a political party to challenge the Democrats at their own convention. Jim Crow finally died with the Civil Rights Act of 1964. And America started a fight it couldn't finish in Vietnam, a country no one knew anything about, and everyone underestimated.

This time, I left Lisa and Priscilla at home with my mama. I was only going for five days and besides my wanting to spare them from their father, I needed a break from them.

And I was flying for the first time.

"I don't know why Anderson can't just come and get you so you can stay on the ground." Mama didn't trust planes. If it were up to her, the only things that would fly were birds and bugs.

"He could drive down, see his babies and have a good meal before y'all head on."

To me, though, flying was freedom. I remember days at the movies downtown, watching white folk board planes to places I couldn't even imagine. They always looked so happy, so polished. They lounged in first class seats with cigarettes and martinis, while flight attendants served cheese and fruit. I was in coach, but that didn't matter nearly as much as being able to fly, to finally get to see the world as white people had gotten to for decades. That plane ticket was the best gift Anderson ever gave me.

"Mama, he just doesn't have the time right now, and flying is much faster. I'll be fine."

I dressed to the nines. Hair pressed, new dress, shoes shining. I looked like I walked straight out of a Cary Grant movie. Back then, everybody looked their best when they got on a plane. The airport looked like a fashion runway, hundreds of people rushing to gates, lounging in restaurants, or smoking in bars in suits, silk scarves, high heels, ties, and pencil skirts. It was like I remembered Harlem, but even fancier. Daddy dropped me off at the closest airport in Columbia and had me pray with him before he let me get on the plane. He was praying for the pilot; I was praying to return without any bruises.

I kept my eyes glued to the window for the whole flight. The clouds were so close, giant cotton balls that brushed up against the plane as it climbed higher into the sky. Below us, the world looked like something out of a snow globe: the roads like painted lines, cars like ants on a farm, the trees like bushels of broccoli. Three hours passed like fifteen minutes and as we lowered back through the clouds, I recognized the flat dustiness of Oklahoma, the farmland, the little wooden houses surrounded by miles of grass and tumbleweed. I was so focused on the window that I didn't pay much attention to what was happening on the plane. The flight attendant seemed uncomfortable serving me water and peanuts, but I don't remember who sat next to me or around me.

The winds were blowing high when I walked off the plane and my hair went flying. I felt like Dorothy Dandridge or one of the Supremes, waiting for my limo while photographers for Time and Life magazines swarmed around me, shooting pictures and calling my name. Instead, I walked straight up to Anderson, waiting in the terminal with his hands in his pockets. I tried a smile, but he just grunted hello, turned around, and started walking toward the baggage claim. For a minute, I was tempted to turn the other way and take the next flight back home. Two things kept me from it: seeing Sadie and the scene I knew he'd make if I tried it.

I looked around me and noticed for the first time the number of army wives that had been on the plane with me. For them, the flight must've been torturous. I watched their husbands in their camouflage uniforms, hugging and kissing their wives, sometimes lifting them clear off the ground while the flight attendants looked on smiling and cheering. Meanwhile, my husband had disappeared around the corner, never once looking back. I slung my carry-on around my shoulder and followed the signs to baggage claim.

I thought we were going back to our house by the base, but he had other plans. When he pulled into the parking lot of a hotel, I asked him why he was spending money instead of just going home.

"I want you all to myself," he said, with that same grin. There was a time when I would've given almost anything to hear him say that. Many nights I dreamt of him taking me in his arms, whispering those very words in my ear and I would submit to his very will, heart racing, filled with the love we shared. It still made my heart race, but this time out of fear. The room was at the corner of the hotel. The door opened from outdoors, and there was a king-sized bed, a nightstand, a lamp, a small bathroom, a sink, and a small black and white television.

My luggage was lost on another plane. I had nothing but the clothes on my back and my handbag, which thankfully held my toiletries. The airline receptionist suggested that we just wait until the other plane arrived, but Anderson wouldn't hear of it.

"That's your shit. Your problem."

I didn't see my suitcase until I left Oklahoma five days later.

The routine was the same every day. He woke up, rolled on top of me, did his business, dressed and left with the key. I showered, washed my underwear, put it up in the window to dry, and paced the room and watched television until he came back, which was usually after seven or sometimes even ten at night. By that time, I'd be starving. By the end of the second day, I had finished all the snacks I brought with me on the plane.

"Anderson, I'm hungry," I'd say. "When are we gonna get something to eat? It won't take long."

"Well I don't know where you gonna get food, but I already ate on the base." He looked at me like I was crazy. I stared right back at him. He knew I couldn't get back into the motel room if I ever left and he never thought to, or rather, never wanted to bring anything back for me. If I argued, I knew it would end in a fight and I'd be too weak to fight back. Every night ended with him back on top of me, my eyes closed while I waited for him to finish. When he finally rolled over and fell asleep, I would go wash him off me. I felt filthy, degraded, trapped. There wasn't enough water or soap to wash away the disgust I felt for him. Afterwards I lay wide awake next to him, my stomach growling wondering where was the man who promised me and my daddy that he would always take care of me?

I couldn't take it anymore. I broke out on the third day. Right after he left, I walked out of the room and let the door lock behind me. I could feel my heart in my throat. I was an escaped prisoner and each step away from that door was terrifying. I kept looking around for him, expecting him to pounce at any second. Three years out of his reach, and I had lost my edge, lost the nerve to fight him head on. I felt cowardly and wise all at once. My fear was almost paralyzing, but it forced me to start using my head.

I gathered myself and marched right up to the motel clerk's desk.

"How may I help you, ma'am?" The woman smiled at me, pink lipstick and slightly crooked teeth.

"Uh, well...my husband's at work and I'm locked out of my room." My heart was still in my throat. It was a risk. They could be watching me for him. I imagined her smiling the same way at Anderson, telling him that she'd caught me trying to escape. My heart beat faster.

"Ma'am?"

"Sorry, what did you say?"

"What's your room number?" She was still smiling.

"131."

"Okay, we'll get you a spare key. Sorry about that."

"Thank you."

"My pleasure."

I found the vending machine and bought all the chips, snack cakes, cookies and orange soda I could handle. The nearest restaurant was over a mile away and I wouldn't dare stray that far. I hid all the food in my bag and threw the wrappers away outside the room when I finished. I brushed my teeth before he came back.

For the rest of our stay, I asked him about food every night, pleading with him, though I knew he wouldn't budge.

"What about Sadie? We were supposed to have dinner with her and James at their house. She was gon' cook."

"I brought you out here for me, not to be gossiping with no females. Do that back in South Carolina. You're on my time now."

Sad as I was to miss Sadie, I was happy that I found a way to beat him without being beaten. And I was going home.

I left the spare key with the housekeeper before we checked out. I waited in the truck while he turned in his key, praying that the clerk wouldn't say anything to him about the spare. When he got back in the truck, he turned the ignition and looked at me for a few seconds. I didn't dare look back.

"Time for you to go."

"Okay."

He pulled out of the parking lot and I kept my eyes straight forward, as if looking back would tell him everything. The further we got away from the hotel, the more I relaxed.

Four hours left. I thought about the army wives who would be on the plane with me that afternoon, how many sad goodbyes would be exchanged at the gate. Figured I'd be the only one of them smiling all the way home.

The sun was high and hot that day. No clouds. Both of us were sweating in the truck, which had no air conditioning, but he refused to roll the windows down, not even an inch.

"I work in this heat all the time. I don't need the air."

I didn't argue. I closed my eyes and leaned against the headrest. I felt the sweat dripping down my back and my forehead. It was at least ninety-five degrees and humid. My tongue and throat were drier than saltines from all the junk I'd been eating and I was starting to feel weak.

Three hours left.

I felt the pickup slow into a turn and I opened my eyes. We were driving into an open field, desert-like, with a giant oak tree that looked out of place. Truly, I felt like we had wandered onto the set of some old country western. All we needed was a couple horses, a lasso, and some cowboy boots. All around, there were warning signs about wild buffalo in the area. "Keep moving," the signs read.

Anderson pulled up beside the tree and cut the engine off. "Where are we?" I asked.

"Mind your business. I'm gon' take a nap before we drive to the airport."

The windows were still rolled up and the truck filled with the smell of cigars and sweat. Anderson's face was soaked in it, but he just wiped it off with his cap, leaned back in his seat and slid the cap over his eyes. I needed air. I opened the door and got out of the truck. Aside from the smell of dung, there was a nice breeze coming off the tree. I shut the door, stretched, and got in the back of the truck. Under different circumstances, I would've thought the place was romantic. The dusty tan of the land was so widespread that you couldn't tell where it ended and the sky began. I started daydreaming about what it would've been like to be here with Anderson if he were the man I thought I married.

We'd have a picnic under the tree or maybe in the bed of the truck. Deviled eggs, chicken, potato salad, homemade rolls and sweet tea. We'd talk about anything and nothing. Our kids, the perfect weather, meeting at the well, our future. We'd stay and watch the sun slip behind the field, and he'd make love to me right there in the bed of the truck under blanket and stars.

I smiled at the thought, lying on the bed of the truck, watching the horizon while he snored away in the cab. I fell off to sleep.

I woke up a few minutes later to a rolling sound in the distance. I saw black. A little speck at first, like a fly landing on a brightly colored painting. Then two. Then four. Then eight. Then a cloud. The dust flew high in the distance and the back of the truck vibrated underneath me.

I stood in the bed of the truck and reached for the handle, trying to open his door, but my hands were too shaky. I banged on the window hard as I could, but he didn't budge. When I leaned over to his side of the cab, he looked right at me through the driver's side window and grinned at me, just like that night on the highway. I backed away from the window, shaking.

The buffalo were coming straight at us, full speed. I froze for a few seconds, looking at how huge they were, how unstoppable. A giant flock of birds shot out of the tree behind me and I backed into the corner of the truck bed, screaming. I was halfway up the roof of the cab when the lead buffalo made a sharp right turn, about 100 yards from me. The rest of the pack followed, and I stood clinging to the roof until the last one was out of sight.

I slid to my knees, thanking God between breaths. Tears and sweat dripped down my face, as I rocked myself back and forth, still shaking.

The driver's door opened and Anderson stepped out of the cab, stretching and grinning. "I bet that scared the shit out of you. Now you'll get ya ass back in this truck." He stretched once more, slid back into his seat and unlocked the door.

I kept the shade down on the plane window, and cried every time I thought about those buffalo. I guess folks figured I was just another army wife, missing her husband.

Chapter 7

ANDERSON'S FAMILY still lived in Paw Creek. His father had died some years before, but his brother and his younger sister were still there, and he dropped in on them every Christmas when he'd come from Oklahoma. Aside from the occasional run-in at the grocery store or passing in the street, I never saw them. And to the best of my knowledge, they never saw me. It wouldn't have mattered if they did. Most of my days were spent taming hair or children; nothing that would make your eyes or ears pop. Yet, my head would get popped good at least once a visit because of something his sister told him she saw while he was away.

"She saw you with a nigger," he'd say, cornering me in the bedroom. "Said you was in his car showin' off around town. Tell me she lyin'."

Of course, I thought *he* was lying. I knew his sister never liked me. But, I didn't or rather, couldn't believe that she was as crazy as him.

"Now why would she say something like that?" I'd say it like I was asking Priscilla about one of her tall tales.

Pop.

One to the head.

Pop.

Another to the chest or stomach.

At home, he was all fist pops. He'd mastered them as if he practiced in a boxing ring somewhere. They were enough to make a point, but not to do any damage. At most I'd get a mild headache, or a bruise where no one could see.

"Call my sister a liar again. I dare you."

For once, he was telling the truth. His sister wrote letters to him. He showed them to me. They told him that she had seen me out with many men while he was away, riding in their cars, walking arm in arm downtown.

"I know those ain't your kids neither," she wrote.

He snatched the letter from me.

Pop. Another to the head.

"We gonna take a paternity test. You not gonna put them girls on me."

"Never been on you anyway."

Pop.

By then, I felt somewhat immune to his accusations. Seemed like every other sentence that came out of his mouth started or ended with "ya nigger" or "them girls ain't mine." Frustrating as it was, I'd learned to ignore it, mostly because I was convinced that he knew the truth. But the paternity test raised the bar on crazy. People said things about girls who needed paternity tests back then. When they weren't talking about the war, the president, or black freedom, there was always a story or two about some love affair gone bad, who was expecting and if she knew the daddy.

If Anderson's sister had spread any of her nonsense around town, I never heard about it. Still, the day I took my children in for the test, I had this paranoia that I was being watched and judged by every pair of eyes that could see me: people in their cars, people walking in and out of the medical center, in the waiting room, in the ladies' room. The doctors, nurses, technicians, all of them just waiting to spread the news that Ella Mae Williams didn't know her own children's father. But I had to prove a point. Back then, paternity tests were not like they are today where they matched the DNA. They only needed to match the blood type to determine paternity. I didn't need either. I knew who my children's daddy was. He didn't have to hit me that day.

"You some lucky bitch," he said after I sent him the results. "You slept with a man with my same blood type."

Nineteen sixty-eight was the last time we spent in Oklahoma. The country was exploding over Vietnam and gradually, soldiers I had come to know at Fort Sill were deployed in droves to kill people—soldiers, old men, women, children—whom they knew only as the enemy. "Charlie." Such a familiar name for "evil" people.

I don't know why he wanted me to live with him again. It would have been pointless and dangerous to question him. Like all good soldiers, I was well prepared for the battle. I knew what to expect from him at Fort Sill. I knew the layout of the house, what corners to avoid, what maneuvers to dodge or lessen the blows. And with two children around, there were fewer times and fewer places in the house where he could fight me openly. Violent as he was, children's eyes were always off limits.

It only lasted five months.

∞

Priscilla and Lisa were school aged, and I was both eager and nervous to let them go out of the house. I was their security and they were mine.

Our days began at 5:30 a.m., when Anderson woke up and got ready for the base. It usually took him thirty minutes to reach the kitchen, where I had to have breakfast waiting for him at the table. Fried eggs, bacon, and buttered toast. If I was late, he complained. If I was too early and something had gotten cold, he complained. If the bread was too toasted or the eggs weren't runny enough, or the bacon wasn't crisp enough, he complained. And if everything was just right, he complained. A few times, he just hit me instead.

"You not gonna get lazy on me," he'd say, walking out the door.

Priscilla and Lisa woke up right after he left. Priscilla would always get Lisa out of bed and rush her into the bathroom, quickly looking both ways as they crossed the hall.

They were soldiers too. It wasn't fair what they had to go through.

Whenever I thought of leaving him, which was often, it was for them. I dreamt about it frequently: keeping them home from school one day after he left for the base, packing their clothes and using money I'd saved to take them on their first plane ride back to South Carolina or New York. But the fantasy always ended there. He was a soldier too, trained far better for the hunt than me. He would find us, and then what? I'd wake up some nights soaked in sweat and tears because of what I imagined would happen next. We couldn't escape, not even to my parents. Not even they could protect me. I was the property of Bill Anderson. It was true that women were fighting for more rights then; everyone was. But battered women had no rights, no shelters, no sanctuaries. Not yet.

And as many women did in my generation, I did the best I could with the lot handed me.

Weekday mornings were sacred times for the three of us. I'd meet them in the bathroom and help them wash up and brush their teeth, and we'd pick out what they were going to wear to school. I started doing hair for women at the base for extra money so I could make sure my girls looked their best. I'd do their hair with curls and colorful bows, and we'd talk and laugh over pancakes and eggs before it was time to walk them to school.

By the time we reached the school grounds, Priscilla's face was more relaxed, and both looked just like all the other girls on the playground—carefree. I prayed it would always be that simple.

I spent most of my days either doing hair or spending time with Sadie. First time I saw her, she grabbed me and gave me the biggest hug, like I was her long-lost child.

"You shouldn't have come back." She stared at me, somber.

"Well, I missed you too, Sadie."

"You know what I mean, Ella Mae. I'm serious. You know I'm happy to see you, but this was the wrong decision."

"What choice did I have? If I stayed, he'd hurt me. He'll hurt me here too, but at least I did what he said. Saying no would have been more dangerous."

"You're afraid of him."

"Wouldn't you be?"

She sighed and looked away for a few seconds. The frustration formed a knot in the middle of my stomach, hot and tight. No one ever raised a hand to Sadie. Never threatened her life. She had nothing to say about my decisions.

She looked back at me, her eyes softer.

"I know I'm not where you are. And maybe it's not my place to say anything, but I'll just tell you something my mother told me. When you act in fear, you're only protecting them."

I stared back at her. The knot was still tight, still hot. "I did what I thought was safest, Sadie."

She nodded.

"Just think about it, okay?"

Afternoons were worrisome. I picked Priscilla and Lisa up from school around three. Anderson was never home when I left, but he'd sometimes be there when we got back, or shortly thereafter. We'd be chatting, the three of us, laughing about what happened in school and as soon as we saw his car in the driveway, we froze. Priscilla's smile would melt from her face. Lisa would put her thumb in her mouth. Both would cling to me.

I'd try to play it off.

"Hey, it's just your daddy, see? It ain't the boogieman."

But to them, he was. They'd never once seen him hit me, but the sound and the aftermath were more than enough. They never looked in his eyes or spoke in his presence, and when they had to walk around him, they kept a wide radius between their bodies and his, running once their backs were to him.

He seemed satisfied with their fear, so much so that I think he felt that he didn't need to touch them. I was grateful for that at least.

Sometimes, if the morning had been rough and the weather was nice, I'd take them for ice cream, just for a delay. I'd look out the windows to make sure he wasn't watching, and then we'd turn around and make our escape. They ate slowly, and I ate too fast. I was always too nervous to enjoy it.

It wasn't so much the beatings that put me on edge. Those were second nature by then. The body can adapt to almost anything. It was my mind that was the problem. No matter what, I couldn't get used to the anticipation that came just before he put his hands on me. Once he began, I was pure adrenaline; my body took over and did exactly what it was supposed to do. Duck. Block. Crouch. Repeat. But my head was never that intuitive. Waiting for that first blow was torture, like the agony before the nurse gives the shot, only a thousand times more insufferable. My imagination ran wild. What *this* time? The head? The chest? The stomach? Fist or open hand? Boots or knees? Choking? Concussion? Would he finally do it? Would he let the girls see my lifeless body? My heart sped up at the thought. How could they ever come back from something like that?

Sadie was right. It was the fear that brought me back to Oklahoma; the fear of the unknown consequences of not letting him have his way.

But losing his game by obeying didn't mean that I'd win by disobeying. I was protecting him, but I was also protecting me, protecting us. For me, there was no glory in dying for a chance at freedom. Unlike the masses I saw fighting and dying together on the news, I knew that my battle belonged to no one else but me. If I died, it would be alone. There would be no one celebrating my rebellion against my husband. There would only be a quiet funeral and a bunch of chatty townsfolk shaking their heads.

"You know it's a shame about Ella Mae. But ya gotta wonder why she'd make him so mad if she knew he was crazy?"

"Dunno, but the real shame is those babies. Just look at them. Lost her over some foolishness."

The evenings were the worst. If he wasn't home when I returned with the girls, he'd be there within a couple of hours. I tried not to let him catch me off guard.

I had laid the girls down in their room for a nap. I went into our bedroom to change clothes before starting dinner. As I pulled my blouse over my head, I felt my arms being pulled back, something he loved to do. The blouse stretched tightly over my face, and I screamed.

"Thought it was your nigger, didn't you?" He laughed softly in my right ear, still tugging my arms. The blouse was cotton, so I could still breathe, but the shock had me gasping for air.

He kept laughing and tugging until he got bored and shoved me onto the bed. I ripped the seam of the shirt trying to get it off and he laughed harder. I covered my heart with one hand and heaved, tears fell and I gasped for air.

"Where's my dinner?" He stopped laughing and stared at me, cold.

Before I could answer, he slapped me across my face.

"A man's supposed to have his dinner waiting for him when he gets home. You been with your nigger and forgot my food. Useless bitch!"

He jumped on top of me and pinned my thighs with his knees. Fists came down on me like hammers, on my arms, my chest, my neck, my face. I tried to block him as best I could, but it only made him angrier. Finally, he'd got worked up to do what I knew he wanted. It was sick foreplay, but he liked it. He kept my legs pinned with his knees while he unbuckled his pants. He exited as forcefully as he entered and released my chaffed, bruised thighs and jumped to his feet, staring at me while he buckled his pants.

"Now get my dinner ready."

∞

The deployments to Vietnam were moving quickly by then. Anderson never talked about it, but I knew he had to be thinking about it. Nam was all anyone ever talked about.

"Won't be long before James will have to go," Sadie said one day on the porch. "I won't know what to do with myself without him."

"Funny," I said, "I'll know exactly what to do if Anderson has to leave."

Independent as she was, Sadie wasn't Sadie without James. And vice versa. The two of them were inseparable. Far as I was concerned, he treated her like royalty. She was free to spend all day with me, getting her hair done if she wanted, going to the mall if she wanted a new blouse or some new perfume. When she left me in the afternoons, I always knew that she was just leaving one best friend to spend time with the other. She smiled like a little schoolgirl when she said his name. "I'ma go see what James is getting into" or "James brought home the best barbeque last night—you want some?"

Just the thought of a man bringing dinner home was enough to make me swoon.

Sometimes after Sadie told me a particularly romantic story, she'd leave and I'd stay out on the porch with my blanket and think back to our courting days, back when I was in love with him. Back when I didn't know to be afraid of him. The visits to the schoolyard, where he'd poke at my curls with a twig, and ask about my studies. The perfume, the dress from Europe. The love letter that never said, "I love you," but said it just the same. For as much as I wanted to believe that it was all genuine, that something changed in him between the time we were engaged and when we married, I couldn't help thinking that it was all just a big lie, a giant trap. I would try to think of ways I could have known, hints he might have given me, but there was nothing before our wedding that would have given even a clue. And even when the signs were glaring at me, the night of our wedding, in the hospital in Connecticut, in the letters he'd write, I was too much in love, too willing to give him the benefit of the doubt to recognize that something was wrong.

And now that I knew, now that the love was a distant memory, there was only fear and habit keeping me there. And tradition. I'd never known a battered wife to escape her husband. Divorces were becoming more common, but country folk like us saw it as a city problem. Fast people losing sight of their morals, losing sight of God. That didn't have anything to do with us.

"Marriage ain't gonna make itself work," Mama would say. "You gotta work it like it's your job."

Abuse was just another trial, another challenge, they'd say. You just gotta find the root of the problem and solve it.

I wondered how Minnie must've felt, hearing people say these things around her. I wondered if she felt like me: angry, patronized, and guilty all at the same time. Guilty that she hadn't been able to solve the problem, even though she knew at her core that she could do nothing to cure the deacon's craziness.

I stayed for eleven more years out of fear, habit and the sickening guilt that comes from being unsuccessful at what seemed effortless to most of my friends, to my own parents.

I was pregnant by November.

I wanted to stay on the base. Paw Creek might have been safer, but my parents were getting older, and I didn't want to put my father through the stress again. Priscilla and Lisa were happy in school, and I didn't want to move them back to those country schools, where they were still fighting over integration. But above all, I wanted to avoid a repeat of the winter drive where I almost lost my child. I didn't think I'd be so fortunate the second time around. I pleaded with Anderson to let me stay and have the baby there.

"There's all these young couples having babies here all the time," I told him. "No reason why we can't do it too."

"You going home. I'm not dealing with no more of ya nigger's babies. Go home to the one that loves you."

"Please, Anderson," I begged. I looked straight into his eyes for what seemed like hours.

"You deaf?" he asked finally. "I said you going home."

He didn't say when. I wasn't going to ask, hoping that he'd just forget about it. But hope didn't stop the nightmares. Every night I'd lay trying to keep my eyes open for as long as possible, terrified of what was waiting for me in my sleep.

We were back on the road in Georgia, snow falling so hard we could barely see. I'd feel the contractions tearing through me. Then the begging— "You got to pull over, Anderson… it's the baby… something's wrong with the baby…" I'd roll out of the car and crawl up that same snowy hill, crying and praying all the way. But then my foot would slip, or my hand would grab something that gave, and I'd go rolling back down the hill, screaming and grabbing for anything to break the fall.

I'd wake up then and cover my mouth because I could never be sure if the screams I heard were real or just in my head. I'd look over at Anderson to see if he heard me, but whiskey never wakes. I never saw what happened next. I didn't need to.

"Well, I don't see how he'd have the time to just be driving you all the way out to South Carolina," Sadie said. "James said they're keeping everyone on base for deployment. He should be getting his papers any day now." She said the last part real quiet, as if doing so would make it less true.

"Bottom line is he ain't gonna put you through that again. Not now. He ain't got the time."

I had a near miss with the baby a few weeks later. I'd just gotten the girls off to school and I was cleaning up after breakfast when a stream of water rushed from between my legs.

"No. No… please, God. Please, no."

I grabbed the bottom of my stomach as the contractions started.

"No no no no. Please God, no. It's too soon, God. Please, it's too soon."

I didn't see it coming. Not a hint. The beatings hadn't changed; he didn't hit me any more than usual. But my body had changed. I called the base, frantic.

"Anderson, please, I gotta go to the hospital …the baby…something's wrong …my water broke … it's too soon."

"I'm at work and you calling me about some nigger's baby. There's always something wrong with your damn babies."

"Anderson, please," I choked, "there's no time for this. You gotta come now, or …"

"If your ass ain't ready by the time I pull up, I'm leaving you right there. Baby be damned."

He hung up.

I only had time to put on my coat and grab my purse before he came speeding up the driveway. I hobbled down the driveway and got in the car and he sped away again before I had a chance to finish shutting the passenger door.

"I'm sick of your shit," he said, ripping through the streets.

I leaned my head against the seat, closed my eyes, and focused all my energy on breathing. We got to the emergency room in five minutes.

"I'll go in and you can park," I said, opening the door.

He looked at me like I'd grown three heads.

"I ain't missing work for nobody, 'specially not you. Find your own way back home."

He leaned over, closed my door, and screeched his way out of the lot.

I couldn't be angry. No energy. I started to feel weak and everything in front of me started to dim. I started shuffling toward the entrance to the emergency room as quickly as I could, when a nurse spotted me from inside and ran out with a wheelchair. I collapsed into it, and he had to straighten me out so I was sitting right.

"Ma'am? Can you hear me, ma'am?"

His voice sounded miles away. I couldn't see him.

"Yes."

"Ok, ma'am, can you tell me what happened?"

I'm not sure I answered him. I woke up in a hospital bed, hooked to an IV and some other machines. I couldn't tell what time it was or what they'd done to me. I put my hand on my stomach, but I couldn't feel anything. Another nurse came into the room then, wearing crisp whites, tights and her cap.

"You're awake," she said cheerfully. "And how are you feeling?"

"My baby," I said, still touching my stomach. "I can't feel my baby." My lip trembled and tears started, slowly at first, and then the flood.

The nurse looked at me, worried. I'll call the doctor in for you," she said and then hurried out of the room.

Two babies slipped away just like that. I couldn't stop crying.

The doctor came in quietly, a tall older man with thick creases in his forehead that showed all his worries. He was one of the first black doctors I'd seen. I thought of Ma Lil, how proud she'd be to see him in his white coat.

"And how are we now?" he asked, looking slightly concerned at my tears.

"I don't know how it happened," I said between heaves. "My water just broke out the blue and I didn't see it coming..."

He came over to me with his stethoscope and put the cupped part down on my belly.

"Yes, well, your body was under tremendous stress, Mrs. Anderson," he said. "It's a miracle that you both made it." He looked up at my face, which froze at 'both.' He smiled at me.

"Just relax now, ma'am," he said. "I gave you an anesthetic for the pain, which is why you probably can't feel your baby right now, but I assure you, it's alive. You've got quite a little soldier in there."

I covered my mouth, and began sobbing again. I felt the tension slowly melt from my body and I started to pray.

"God, thank you, thank you for bringing us this far. Please keep us fighting to stay alive; please let us make it through. Thank you. Thank you. Thank you."

Sadie and James picked up the girls from school and kept them at their house while they monitored me at the hospital for the next few days. Sadie visited every day with stories about how they were getting along, how school was going, and such, but I asked her not to bring them or to tell them where I was because I didn't want to scare them.

"Ella Mae," she said during one visit, "I told myself I was gonna stay out of this, but this scare snapped me out of it."

She looked at me, her eyes real serious and grabbed my hands in hers.

"Even if it takes a while, you gotta get yourself out of this mess with him." Her eyes started watering a bit, but she shook it off and looked at me more intensely. "You can't keep this up," she said. "Not you, not your babies. If you don't get out, it will kill you. He will kill you. Please don't let him win."

I didn't know what to say. I knew she was right, but I couldn't form the words to respond. I just nodded.

They released me from the hospital a few days later in the early afternoon. Sadie picked me up and we went together to get the girls from school. They ran up to me, pigtails flying and held on tight to me. On the drive home, they showed me everything they'd done in school that day, chatting loudly and giggling.

He was home, waiting for us. As usual, the girls froze.

"C'mon now, girls," Sadie said softly, "let's help your mama get into the house."

They followed her out the car and walked in front of me to the door. Anderson was waiting in the kitchen, holding some papers in his hand.

"Afternoon, Anderson," Sadie said as cordially as she could.

He nodded at her and shifted his eyes to me. I set my bag down on a chair in the kitchen and the girls ran off to their room.

"You okay?" Sadie asked. I could tell she didn't want to leave me there.

"Yeah, Sadie. I'll be all right now. Thank you for everything."

She gave me a tight hug.

"I'll come see about you in the morning."

"Alright then, girl. See ya then."

She shut the door quietly behind her. Anderson looked at me, smirking. He threw the papers down on the table.

"They're sending me to Vietnam," he said proudly. "And now you got to go home."

This time, I didn't argue.

Chapter 8

HE SHOULD have never gone to war.

I watched the reports on television every night. Everyone did. I saw the lists of the dead, the photos of the injured, all blown off limbs and broken minds. The war ads and state speeches fooled no one—people were being sent to a country no one knew anything about to be killed or maimed for a cause most of us weren't convinced was worth the cost. Every now and then, I'd see a name or two on the casualty list that I knew from Fort Sill and I'd try my best to send letters to the wives, even though I felt like nothing I could say would be comforting. What do you say to someone whose world has been shattered? Army wife or not, nothing prepares a woman for that kind of loss, that kind of pain. To know that your husband, perhaps even the love of your life, took his last breath in a place that wasn't home and was in so much pain that death was merciful. To hear so many of your countrymen, maybe even your friends and family, say that it was all for nothing, all for an agenda that was never yours, or his, was too unbearable to speak of. But I tried nonetheless.

Sadie and I kept in touch with letters every now and then. James was deployed around the same time as Anderson, and she stayed behind in Oklahoma to wait for him to come home. He was all she could talk about.

"I miss him so much, Ella Mae," she wrote. "I keep waiting for them to come to my house with their flag and sorrys. My heart sinks to my shoes every time there's a knock on the door."

Try as I might, I couldn't empathize. I was happy.

∞

Anderson sent us back to South Carolina on a plane and I got to watch my girls squealing and squirming in excitement as we took off into the clouds. Priscilla loved it. She kept staring out the window and pointing at all the different kinds of clouds as they passed, wondering why we could just fly through them like they weren't there. Lisa liked it too, but I could tell she was a bit scared about being so far off the ground. She smiled and giggled a lot, but wouldn't look out the window again after we took off. Neither liked the ear popping, but they sat through it like the soldiers they were, never complaining.

Sadie was right. The deployment happened so fast that Anderson had to get rid of us as quickly as he could.

Going home felt like defeat at first. The look on my mother's face when we got back to Paw Creek said more than any words could. I was a single mother, alone with two children and one on the way. I was failing at marriage. It was true. But as the plane put more and more miles between us and him, the release of tension in my body, in their bodies, made that fact feel less like a problem and more like a solution. It wasn't ideal, but it was safe. And that was all we needed.

Anderson was gone for one year. He left right before the holidays in November. It was the first time in ten years that I enjoyed the holidays. Everyone noticed.

"Ella Mae, you sure taking this Vietnam thing mighty well," they'd say, half-laughing, half-wondering if I'd lost my mind.

I just smiled.

"You know, I just got this feeling like God's gonna take care of everything. He's gonna take care of Anderson and we're all gonna be fine."

"Amen," they'd say, grinning.

Hattie noticed too, only she knew the truth.

"Freedom is a good thing, Mae," she said to me one night after dinner. "Good for you and them babies."

I looked at her and instantly felt the guilt. I knew what was at stake, him being at war, and I did worry from time to time, but I didn't feel it like the other wives. I couldn't. How could I reveal the many nights I sat up thinking, maybe hoping, there was a knock at the door and two uniformed officers were standing there to deliver the news. Then my nightmare would end. My children would not remember the evil they called father. They would only remember the stories I invented about the war hero who died trying to protect his country. I'd pray for forgiveness. No one should ever wish someone dead. It was a way out.

"I don't want anything bad to happen to him," I said, trying to avoid eye contact.

"Oh, don't worry about that," she said. "They just don't know the truth of it, is all. They think you ought to be all tears and sleeplessness, wishing he was home for the holidays. You just enjoy this time. Leave the rest to God."

I never had to tell Hattie anything. She'd sensed the danger in him long before he raised a hand to me. I remembered everything she'd said to me about self-reliance; about making sure that I never became dependent on any man for anything. It was the most valuable advice I'd ever gotten.

That Christmas was Hattie's last. She died of breast cancer just after my third baby, Maxine was born. Like Ma Lil, she went too swiftly for any of us to realize what was happening. I remember talking to her on the phone the day before she died. I was supposed to do her hair that week, but she said she wanted me to wait.

"I want you to do my hair up real pretty next week," she said. "I know you'll do it right."

"But you not gon' be up here next week."

"Yeah, I will. And I want you to do it pretty for me."

"Alright, Hattie. Whatever you want."

"And Ella Mae?"

"Yeah?"

"Remember everything I told ya, right?"

"Yeah, Hattie."

Hattie and I never talked much, but when we did, it was as if we talked every day, like me and Sadie. She could tell so much just by looking at me and listening to how I said things.

Her death hit me particularly hard, not just because she'd been so supportive, but also because we'd become so close. Hattie belonged to a generation of my parents' children to whom I was just known as "Lil Mae." She was the oldest girl, and was almost out on her own, school teaching when I was twelve years old. She was like another mother to me. I'd see her during the holidays and whenever she'd come up from her place in Charleston, and she'd talk to me and discipline me as if I were her daughter. She married only once, to a man who really cared for her and their daughter. He never remarried.

We buried her in Charleston, the town she loved so much she could barely stand to leave it. My mama, who took her death harder than all of us, didn't like the idea of her baby being buried so far from home.

"I want her to be where I can see her," she said at the gravesite. "I don't want her thinking we forgot her."

"Hattie's not just gonna be here, honey," my daddy said. "She's gonna be wherever you need her, whenever you need her." He wrapped his arms around her as she wept.

I held on to that thought as tightly as Mama did that day. I still do.

The end of the year was a turning point for our country, and for my life, though neither was aware of it. Four months into the new year, cities across the country erupted in violence and destruction. Martin Luther King, Jr., a man who represented to blacks and whites alike the promise of a better nation, was assassinated while standing on the balcony of a motel in Memphis. Among the things he opposed before he died, was the war in Vietnam, which didn't work with his vision of peace, international brotherhood, and basic Christian morals that our country had forgotten.

We all cried for him, for us. There was a sense of hopelessness that we all felt, that we could see all over the news reports. City streets were filled with folk who agreed and disagreed with King's philosophy, both groups angry that even the best of us, the most educated, the preachers of love in the face of violence and hate, could be shot down like niggers.

Talk of the draft was at everyone's dinner table, and young men were getting scared. If they hadn't thought much about college before, they started to. Others made more creative plans to dodge—shooting themselves in the legs, the arms, anything they could do without to avoid what they were convinced was certain death. Others planned to change their names, to flee to Canada. Anderson never said much to let on what he thought about anything, besides women, but knowing how he thought, I knew he saw them as shameful cowards, hardly men.

But I couldn't blame them. Dying for a country that barely saw you as human, much less a hero, seemed meaningless and wasteful, even if the purpose was worthy.

∞

He should never have gone to war.

The end of the year was the last time I knew Bill Anderson as I'd come to know him in eleven years as his wife. He'd been violent, cruel, and hateful, but he'd also been equally predictable and clear headed, if not rational.

When he left America, I would've called him a monster, a bonafide woman hater because of the way he treated me and talked about women.

When he returned, he was a demon straight from hell, confused, angry, and deadly.

I couldn't tell from the letters. There weren't many, but he sounded the exact same as he always did: suspicious, irritated. When Maxine arrived in May, he said the same thing he did when I had Priscilla and Lisa, "I don't make girls."

Predictable as time itself.

I didn't spend too much of mine thinking about what was happening to him. For once, I thought that mean spirit in him was doing some good—maybe shielding him from the madness that the other soldiers were feeling.

The next six months passed in complete oblivion. Maxine wasn't very fussy, so I slept soundly every night. Priscilla and Lisa fell out of defense mode. They laughed more and played more and doted on their new little sister, who had no reason to be defensive, not yet.

It was peace time. We took advantage of every minute. The summer was full of barbecue, bathing suits and water hoses, ice cream and music. Sometimes at night, after I'd tuck them in or read them stories, they'd ask when their daddy was coming back.

"Sometime soon, I think," I always told them. In the back of my mind, I didn't care if he never came back. I repented.

I prayed. I asked God twice every day to help me find the best way out for us. I asked Him to take care of Anderson, to bring peace to all of us.

When I'd pray these things, I'd often think about those countries like Vietnam, which hadn't known peace for years, even decades. I wondered how they survived it, particularly the women. My only battle was with my husband; they struggled against whole groups of people, many of them perfect strangers. I did feel blessed in that way, in knowing that most places outside my home were safe, that I could be free anywhere else. But what did it say when you couldn't be free in your own house? I supposed many of those women wouldn't envy me either.

He wrote to tell me he'd be back in a couple of weeks. It was early November by then. Priscilla had started the fourth grade and Lisa was in first grade. I remember being home with Maxine when the letter came. I rocked her back and forth as I read it, the anxiety creeping up my body for the first time in months. Maxine looked up at me, as if she felt it too. She was almost six months by then, wide-eyed and smiling all day long. I looked back at her and made faces until she smiled again.

I got a letter from Sadie a few days later. "He's comin' home, Mae! Praise Jesus!!! I better start cooking now, cuz you know we gonna have a feast when he gets here!"

Once again, try as I might, I couldn't empathize. There would be no celebration here.

∞

He stayed in Paw Creek for a day or two, mostly sleeping and eating and going out to wherever. I never asked. Priscilla and Lisa stayed to themselves, quiet and out of his way. Maxine was always on my hip, in the crib, or with her sisters.

He went back to Fort Sill after Thanksgiving, and we went back to how we were, at ease. I watched him leave for the airport, convinced that he was the same man he'd been a year before. I saw no evidence that he wasn't.

Christmas Eve found me staring down the barrel of a loaded pistol.

We were at my mother's house, the five of us, my parents, and some of my brothers and sisters. Everyone seemed so happy, including Anderson. We all thanked him for his service to our country, and celebrated his safe return. Mama had cooked up a storm, and everyone had eaten so much, we all felt like we were about to burst. As we were about to leave the house, I asked Anderson if he could bring the car around to the front of the house. The sleet was coming down thick outside, and I didn't want to have to carry the baby through it. He looked at me like I was crazy.

"You ain't sugar, and neither is that baby," he said. "None of y'all gon' melt."

I felt the familiar heat rise in my face. Part of me was angry with myself for forgetting, even for a second, who he was. It was such a small favor to ask, on a day when he should've been especially thankful to be alive to do it. His smile and laughter that night felt so genuine, it seemed like his heart was open to kindness. My family certainly believed it. But I should have known better.

"Lisa and Prissy, stay here please. I'm going out to the car, and I'll come back around to get you, okay?" They obliged but their shoulders were tense and their eyes worried.

I put a blanket over Maxine's head, and slammed the door. The cold air stung against my burning cheeks and I walked as fast and carefully as I could through the slush.

"Wait, Mommy!" A tiny voice cried out behind me.

Lisa ran out, carrying her baby doll covered with a blanket. The sight of her almost made me forget to be mad. She watched everything I did with Maxine, and had to do the same with her doll. She changed her diapers, fed her a bottle, rolled her through the store with the pink stroller I got her. I waited for her to catch up, and we walked down the driveway to the car. I opened the trunk to put Maxine's things inside, not paying attention to anything except keeping the baby warm.

Lisa saw it first and screamed. I looked up, and there he was, pistol aimed right at my head.

"I'm gon' end it now," he said. "I'm tired of your shit. Don't you know you almost broke the window outta your mom's door slamming it like that?"

His face was so calm, as if we were just having a conversation about the weather, or what we were going to do in the morning. I gripped Maxine to me. Lisa ran with her baby back into the house.

I should've been terrified. I guess part of me was. But the anger hit me so forcefully that I felt nothing but my blood pressure rising, adrenaline pumping. I looked right in his eyes, just as calm as he was.

"Only thing I hate was that your neck wasn't in it," I said. I slammed the trunk shut, still holding Maxine to me. "What you wanna do? You wanna kill me, or you wanna kill me and the baby?"

He said nothing, still pointing the pistol at my head. It just made me angrier. I put Maxine in the back seat of the car and shut the door, facing the pistol.

"So how you wanna do it? You gonna shoot me in the heart, the head or the ass? Or should I turn around and let you shoot me in the back?"

I could hear my heart beat in my ears then. We must've been a sight there in the slush, facing each other down like in some old country western.

"You a coward if you don't," I said. "I'm tired of just dying a slow death with you. Hurry up and get it over with."

It seemed like we stood there forever. I couldn't feel the cold or the wet falling on my face, my hair. My feet were planted in the ground like a stubborn bull, and with each passing second, I felt myself get stronger and angrier. I wanted him to do it. I wanted him to finally show everyone who he really was.

"You do it, or your daddy's a bastard."

The door to the house opened again, and he lowered the pistol from my face. I was still staring at him, waiting.

"Y'all okay out there?" Mama called out to us. "I got these babies bundled up for you. They ready to go."

Just as I thought. He could have easily killed me right there in front of my family. That wasn't his goal. He wanted to spend his days torturing, humiliating me until I had no choice but to take my own life to get away from him, to have peace. He didn't know me very well. I had my girls to live for and I wasn't leaving them to be raised by an animal. If I had to be the one tortured so they could live free, I volunteered to be the scapegoat to protect them.

∞

What they called Post-Traumatic Stress Disorder, or PTSD, didn't exist in the late '60s. In fact, it was something that no one spoke about, even though we know now that it was very common, especially for war vets. I think today of all the women, the army wives, who suffered through this with me during Vietnam, traumatized husbands who carried out the violence they saw against us, our children, and often themselves. There were times when we could identify the triggers, something we said or did that put them right back on the battlefield, players in a ruthless game of kill or be killed. We'd learn to avoid them, to teach our children, our extended families to avoid them. But it was never enough to just stop the triggers. The mind does what it will, when it will. Back then, far more so than now, we just had to pray that we weren't in the way when the episodes occurred.

The last time Sadie wrote to me, she spent a couple paragraphs telling me how wonderful it was to have James home, but two full pages about how much he'd changed.

"I think something's broken in him," she said. "He doesn't smile or laugh, not like he used to. I don't know what I can do. I feel so helpless sometimes. I hope things are at least a bit better for you."

Hardly.

I spent the next ten years dodging two enemies: Anderson, the husband and Anderson, the veteran. I admit that it was hard at times to tell the difference between the two.

When your husband has threatened your life both before and after going to war, you had to measure the nature of each threat by the situation, the way it's made, and the look on his face when he makes it.

In general, I knew that Anderson, the husband liked to attack me in private, away from witnesses, especially children. He was the man who boasted to me that no one would ever believe me if I said he was abusive, because he had a "split personality."

Anderson, the veteran attacked anywhere, at any time, and mostly out of paranoia. His attacks were more extreme than they'd been before Vietnam, and generally came after some odd behavior—a crazed look, random talking as if he didn't know where he was, or moving around as if he were on a battlefield, crouched low or crawling or rushing from one corner of the room to another.

There were plenty of times, though, when he was both at the same time. That first Christmas after Vietnam was one of them.

I stood in the kitchen preparing the holiday meal when I looked out the window and noticed him pacing back and forth across the yard. His hunting rifle was perched on his shoulder. I wiped my hands on my apron and opened the door. I heard him mumbling but didn't understand what he was saying.

"Anderson," I called out to him.

He stopped for a moment looked my way, his eyes stretched wide. He started marching again, every step rough and deliberate. He jumped as if something had startled him. He lowered the rifle and ran toward the bushes.

Not knowing anything about PTSD, I followed him. I reached the edge of the trees when I felt him grab me. I fell to the ground with him on top of me. I trembled and braced myself for what I knew was coming.

We wrestled. I dodged many blows to my face, but they were followed by hits to my stomach and legs. He had rage I had never seen before. His eyes were distant and full of fire. He was yelling, but I couldn't understand what he was saying. Finally, I screamed.

"Anderson," I yelled. My arms in front of my face to block the blows. "Anderson, you're going to kill me in front of our children."

The blows stopped. He held my wrists and looked around as if it was only at that point he realized he was in Paw Creek, in our back yard with our now crying children standing in the doorway. His breathing leveled. He released me and backed away.

I stood. Dirt and bruises covered my body. Pain enveloped me. I spotted the gun laying on the ground beside him and had the urge to pick it up and end all of this. But the sound of whimpering from the house reminded me of the greater call on my life. I limped back to the house and never spoke of it even as family and friends arrived for the holiday.

But regardless of who he was at any given time, the fact is that he beat me whenever he got the chance, sometimes more than once a day. I fought back more than I ever had, but the satisfaction of bruising him as he did me wore off as the fatigue set in. My kicks and punches became more reflexive than aggressive. The only time I got time to heal was when he was away at Fort Sill, which, as his time in the army came to an end, was rare.

As the last years of the '60s passed away, and Vietnam became more of a losing battle, our war at home became full time and uncontrollable. I'd been drafted, just as many young men had been from every corner of the nation. We were terrified, but resigned to our fates.

It had been easy to keep most of this from my parents, at least to some extent. They knew that he'd hurt me before—they saw some of the bruises and witnessed the tension. But they hadn't heard it from me, and more importantly, they wanted to stay out of my marriage.

I wasn't sure how to talk to them about it, but I knew that I had to do it. There were weeks when I'd avoid coming out of the house so they wouldn't see the swollen lip or the black eye. I wasn't going to lie for him, and I needed to be able to say exactly what was happening.

The day I finally told them was after a particularly bad fight at home. Anderson, the husband was upset over a meal I'd cooked and decided to give me a black eye. I took the girls over to see Mama and Daddy the next afternoon. They were both silent, looking at me, but their eyes told me everything. Mama grabbed a towel, filled it with ice cubes, and made me sit down. I sent Priscilla and Lisa out to play, and held Maxine in my lap.

I told them just about everything: the daily beatings, the incident with the buffalo, the long crawl up the snowbank in Georgia. I told them how it'd gotten worse since Vietnam, how he was more irrational, more brutal. I started to cry.

"I've tried everything," I said, holding the ice to my eye. "Nothing's worked in twelve years. I don't know how to make it better for us."

I glanced at them. Daddy was frozen in his chair, wringing his hands. Mama was tearing up, and grabbed tissues for both of us. I'd never known of a problem they couldn't solve together, but I could tell that this one was too much for them, for their time. They looked helpless.

"Ella Mae," Mama said finally, "You got to stop talking about it. Whatever happens in the house got to stay in the house, you hear? Just go back to your husband and work it out."

There was no use in arguing. I just nodded and kept nursing my eye.

Daddy stayed frozen. I still don't understand why. He'd dealt with marital problems, including abuse, with his congregants for years, sometimes successfully. But he seemed almost paralyzed at that table, looking at me. I could tell that he was worried, scared even, but it was like he couldn't form the words to say so, couldn't think of how to make it better.

What he did do was take me to the emergency room. A few times a month, Anderson would hit me so hard on my head that I would need to see a doctor. One of the girls or I would call him wherever he was, and he'd come get me to take me over there. He'd sit and hold my hand while we waited for the doctor. As usual, he didn't say much, but he'd stay with me through everything, making sure I was well enough before taking me home. That was the most time we ever spent together, in the hospital. Shameful as it was, I was so happy to have him always there for me. I didn't understand why he wouldn't do more to try to protect me, but I understood enough to know that he was doing all he felt he could do.

The beatings took a toll on my health and on the girls' spirits. Thankfully, he kept his hands off them, even during his traumatic episodes. But his presence alone terrified them so much that they would shake and run away from him if he came anywhere close to them.

My head injuries developed into migraines so painful I couldn't keep any food down. I'd leave Maxine with Mama and spend days in bed, taking handfuls of painkillers and trying to sleep it off before he got home in the evenings.

The girls would run in to see me after school, climbing up on the bed beside me. I'd keep my eyes closed to shut out the light in the doorway.

"Mommy, you're gonna be okay, right?" Lisa would ask, tearing up.

"Yes, baby," I'd say, reaching out for her hand. "I'm just having a headache day. It'll be all better soon."

"We promise we'll be good," Priscilla said one day.

"You are good, honey," I said to them. "You both are the best I could ask for."

"Then why does he still hit you?" Priscilla started to cry.

I opened my eyes and looked at them. Prissy was about twelve by then, and Lisa was eight. They had gotten tall on me, long skinny brown legs, lanky arms, and thick wavy hair. They were just beautiful. Whether he claimed them or not, they were the only good thing to come from our marriage.

I gestured for both to come closer to me. I placed an arm around them.

"Now I want you to listen good, hear? What happens with me and your daddy has nothing to do with you—"

"Why doesn't he love us?" they asked.

I paused for a while before answering that question. It occurred to me that I didn't think Anderson was capable of loving anyone. Even if I'd given him three sons, he would've found something wrong with them to blame on me. He would have ignored them too.

"Your daddy does love you," I said finally. "Like I said, he's just an angry person and has a hard time showing love. Pray for him, okay?"

They both nodded, unconvinced.

THE AFTERMATH OF LOVE AND WAR 111

Chapter 9

ANDERSON, the veteran appeared more and more as months, and then years progressed. The trauma from the war weighed so heavily on him that he'd spend whole weeks back on the battlefield. I'd wake up at night and find him lying on his stomach in the corner of the bedroom, eyes wide, bloodshot and terrified. I learned the hard way that I shouldn't bother with him when he was in that state, so I'd always lay still and awake, watching him from the corner of my eye until he finally realized where he was and came back to bed.

He didn't shower during those weeks. The stench of his body would fill every room he entered, and we'd try as best we could not to breathe, especially at the dinner table.

Our bedroom was unbearable. He'd climb into bed in clothes he'd been wearing for two to three weeks, soiling the sheets I had to wash every day. He liked to force himself on me at night, pinning me underneath him, his breath smelling of rotting eggs, his body rank as an overused latrine.

I asked him repeatedly to please shower, for his own health. Before Vietnam, he was a stickler for hygiene. He never left the house without a hot shower, a shave, and clean, freshly pressed clothes.

"If I can stay in Vietnam without bathing, I should be able to do the same in my own house," he'd say, his teeth yellow as a school bus.

One night after one of my headache days, Anderson grabbed me across the bed, and started pulling me under him. It'd been about a month since he'd showered, and I couldn't stomach it any longer.

"Get off me," I said sharply, my head pounding.

"What did you say to me?" he spoke directly in my face and I gagged.

He slapped me across my face. My head was ringing and I tried to block his next move, but I felt too weak.

"Who the hell you think you are?" he screamed in my ear. I started to feel faint.

He grabbed me off the bed and shoved me to the floor.

"This is my house, bitch," he said. "You do what I say!"

Suddenly, he went into a coughing fit, like he'd choked on his own words. He let my left hand go for two seconds. I seized the moment and his penis.

He screamed and fell over on the floor. I tried hard as I could to detach his ole peter weatherbird and hickory nuts from his body. I squeezed and jerked, and he made sounds I thought only wild animals could manage.

"Let go! Please! Please, let go!"

The more he pleaded, the harder I pulled. I lifted myself to my knees and hovered above him, staring at him as I pulled.

"Do you know any prayers, Anderson?" I said calmly. I could barely feel the pain in my head for the adrenaline rushing through me. I was winning.

He kept screaming and I just kept pulling.

"I want you to say your prayers, Anderson," I said to him. "I want you to say them for me, backwards and forwards." I felt empowered.

"LORD, please let go! Please let go!"

I think I must've pulled for what felt like ten minutes before I finally let him go, satisfied that he couldn't get back up. He laid twisted in a ball for the rest of the night and I got back in bed, smiling. I put him out of commission for several months.

∞

Nineteen seventy-three was a big year for my family. Anderson was discharged from the army and moved back to Paw Creek full time. He got a teaching position at a technical college, which occupied his days. My parents made it through fifty years of marriage and Priscilla and Lisa were both self-proclaimed teenagers. By all accounts, they were typical for their age—absentminded, silly, self-centered at times. But they were anything but carefree. They were painfully aware at that point that their home life was very different than that of other girls their age. Some of their friends were "daddy's girls," something they couldn't even begin to imagine for themselves, aside from the affection my daddy showed them. Their friends went on vacations, picnics, and church all together as a family. They'd never seen or heard their parents in anything more than little arguments over things that they'd all forget in an hour or two.

Much as I tried to do for them myself, I knew that I couldn't make up for what went on in our house. Thankfully, they never held it against me, not even when their friends showed off all the things they had that my girls didn't have, leaving them to wonder what was wrong with their family.

I was happy that I still had a little one running around. We all shielded Maxine from him as much as possible, now that he was around all the time. She spent a lot of time at my parents' house, especially when Anderson was in vet mode.

She still had that same smile, which made us all feel much better.

My parents' 50th wedding anniversary celebration was one of the biggest parties we'd had since my wedding. Most of the family was there, a lot of them coming down from up North. There were family, friends, neighbors and church folk, all hanging out in the front yard, eating barbecue, drinking Kool-Aid—what we called "penny drink" back then, and chatting up a storm.

Anderson was there too, behaving normally, a smile planted on his face for everyone, especially my parents. My daddy was polite to him, but not nearly as affectionate as he'd been a few years before, which was comforting to me. But Mama took the "killing him with kindness" approach. She still hugged him like a son, insisting that he sit and relax while she fixed him a plate, which he ate clean, and joined the other men who were drinking in the back of the house.

While the girls were playing out in the yard, I sat with an old girlfriend from Fort Sill, whose husband had been re-stationed at Fort Jackson, near Paw Creek. We caught up with each other, exchanging stories about where we'd been, and I introduced her to my family and friends. We were talking about my parents, how amazing it was that they'd made it for fifty years and joking about whether they'd be "making whoopee" that night, when Anderson came up to us, demanding to know what was so funny.

"I don't know what you so happy for, cuz I'd never in hell stay with you for no fifty years," he said, smirking at me. "Fifty years with one woman? Shit, no. Not me." And he walked away.

We were both too embarrassed to say anything.

She and I left the party a few minutes later. We couldn't find anything else to laugh about. She wished me the best and I did the same, and we said our goodbyes. I went straight home afterwards, and cried for the next couple of hours in our bed.

It wasn't that what he said surprised me. He'd said nastier things before. Besides the humiliation, I was upset because he'd pointed out a fact that I'd tried my best not to think about: I'd never know the kind of loving, long-term marriage that my mother had. It was what I wanted for myself more than anything, and he'd thrown it in my face.

The girls ran back in the house at around eight, happy and out of breath from playing all afternoon. They brought me a couple plates from the party and some cake. I told them they could eat the cake and sat in the kitchen with them while they shared it, giggling and hyper from all the sugar.

Seemed like Christmas came in a blink that year. Besides the usual routine, the beatings, trips to the ER, doing hair when I could, I don't recall much of what happened between July and December, except that Priscilla and Lisa were begging me to take them shopping in Columbia for new clothes. Naturally, they'd become obsessed with clothes, almost overnight. They were into the bell-bottoms, the floral print shirts, the platform shoes, which I wouldn't let them wear until they were fifteen or sixteen.

There was a shopping center in Columbia where we liked to go for bargains. We would always go there around Christmastime, but he rarely bought anything for the girls. I did most of the shopping for the family, and he'd sometimes give me money for that.

Because it was the girls' first shopping trip as teens, I wanted to make it extra special for them. Maxine still believed in Santa, so we let her stay with Mama and Daddy so we could pick her gifts out while we were there.

Columbia was about an hour's trip, a much bigger town than what the girls were used to, so they were very excited to be going for a shopping spree. Anderson didn't say much on the way there, which I took as a good sign. He didn't have to be happy about going. I just wanted him to do right by the girls.

But about ten minutes before we arrived at the mall, I could tell he was starting to get irritated. I indulged him.

"What's wrong, Anderson?" I asked gently. "You look like something's bothering you."

The girls got quiet in the back seat, pretending like they weren't there.

"I'm wastin' too much of my damn money on those girls," he said. "That's what's wrong."

We pulled up to the shopping center and parked.

"Well, I'm sorry you feel that way, Anderson, but you know, it's Christmas now. They've been lookin' forward to this for months."

He opened the door and got out of the car. The girls and I jumped out after him, and surprisingly, they went up to either side of him, grabbing playfully at his coattails.

"C'mon, Daddy, it'll be fun," they said, grinning at him. "Just come in with us."

He seemed like he was thinking about it, so I thought I'd give him some more encouragement. I came up behind him and gently grabbed his arm.

"C'mon now, Anderson," I said. "We promise this won't take long."

He jerked away from me, as if I'd attacked him from behind. The girls gasped and stepped back. He looked at me and shoved me backward.

There were a couple of screams from passersby as I fell backward. I twisted my leg to keep from falling, and felt a snap at the bottom of my foot. I balanced myself on the hood of a car, and stood up again. The heel of my shoe snapped off, and was dangling from the bottom.

Everyone stood still for a few seconds, stunned. They looked at me and then at Anderson, who just stood there like nothing happened. The girls were holding on to each other by the mall entrance, crouching as if he were about to come after them too.

"Are you alright, ma'am?" one of the nearby men asked.

I looked over at him and forced a smile.

"Yes, I'm okay, thank you," I said. "It's just a shoe."

People walked slowly away, back to their cars, down the street, into the mall. Too angry to be embarrassed, I put my purse back up on my shoulder, and limped back to the car. The girls followed and then Anderson got in and drove away. None of us said anything until we got to my uncle's house in Columbia, where we stopped to say a quick hello.

He gave us a warm greeting. Happy to see us he hugged the girls and commented on how big they'd gotten. My uncle greeted Anderson with a firm handshake and gave me a kiss on my cheek as we walked inside.

"What y'all doing out this way?" he asked, inviting us to sit.

The girls looked at each other, and then at me. They'd asked for so little from me, from both of us. It made me sick to see how disappointed they were.

"We were just doing some shopping," I said before Anderson could say anything.

We chatted for a while, about forty-five minutes, about everything from family to the war to the weather until my uncle stopped us to turn up his radio. There was a hurricane on the coast that sparked tornado warnings in the area.

"This storm is looking mean," he said. "I think y'all ought to just stay here for tonight or just wait till it blows over."

He looked over at Anderson as he said it, nodding for confirmation. Anderson just shook his head.

"I'm heading back tonight," he said. "And my family's coming with me."

My uncle looked at Anderson and then to the girls and me.

"Now, Anderson, I don't think that's a good idea at all," my uncle said, his voice firmer. "That storm is coming right on your path, and believe me, you don't wanna be caught in that mess."

Anderson looked over toward us and stood up from his chair.

"Thanks for telling us about the storm," he said, "but we're gonna get on the road now."

"Look now, Anderson—" He held out his hand to him.

"We're going. It's my call and I know what to do. Don't you worry."

He shook my uncle's hand and started toward the door. He looked over at us, still sitting in the living room. We got right up and started putting on our coats and hats.

"Please be careful," my uncle said, hugging the girls and me. "Remember to take cover if anything comes at you. Call when you get home, please."

"We will," I said, hugging him. "Thank you for everything. Merry Christmas."

"Merry Christmas, y'all. Be careful."

We rode away from Columbia in total silence, Anderson with his eyes on the road, and us with our eyes at the gray and black sky.

Several miles into the trip, the wind and rain had gotten so severe, we could barely see the road. Tree branches were flying across the two-lane highway, and trash and pebbles from the side of the road kept hitting against the car.

But Anderson wouldn't stop. He rolled down his window and stuck his head out so he could see the road better. The girls were silent in the back seat, wide-eyed and still, holding hands. I reached back to them, and they grabbed my arm.

We made it only a couple more miles before the road was washed out. The water had gotten too high for Anderson to control the car and we started floating down the highway, the winds blowing us back and forth to either side of the road.

Lisa started crying first. Then Priscilla. They leaned forward and grabbed me around the neck, asking me if we were gonna die. I grabbed their arms with both my hands and started talking to them.

"No babies, we're not gonna die," I said. "God is gonna take care of us now, okay? You'll see."

I turned to look at Anderson, who seemed to be enjoying himself, steering the car like it was a boat on a river. I could've strangled him right then.

"What are we gonna do if we see the tornado coming for us?" I asked.

He looked over at us and just laughed. "What we gonna do?" he grinned. "Well I don't know about you and your girls, but I'm gonna get the shit outta here and find a ditch to lay in. You got to figure out what you and your girls are gonna do."

He kept laughing and steering like some evil villain in a horror movie, and we kept clinging to each other until finally, about ten minutes later, the wind and water calmed down, and we hit dry road. It was a miracle that he got the car to start back up.

When we finally got home, we were so shaken up, we could barely talk. I went to the girls' room as they were getting ready for bed, still sniffling.

"You see how God kept us, just like we asked Him to?"

They nodded.

"Everything's gonna be okay."

They kept the nightlight on for the first time in a while. When I finally settled down in bed, he rolled over on top of me, pinning my arms with his hands.

"You see? You almost got us killed in the storm," he said.

I stared back at him, shaking.

"You caused all of this," he continued. "If you hadn't made me go with you and your girls, they wouldn't have been screaming and crying during the storm. You always causing problems."

I wanted to spit in his face. He tried to undress me, but I slapped him instead. Come morning time, I wasn't the only one black and blue.

Christmas had never been special to him. Often, he would leave early Christmas morning to spend the day with his brother and would return after eleven or midnight. He did nothing for me or the girls. I always tried to make the day special for the children buying them special gifts and visiting family on the holidays.

One Christmas, I convinced Anderson to take me and the girls to see the Christmas lights in McAdenville, North Carolina. It was a small town about an hour away that was famous for its city-wide Christmas display. Although he protested, he drove us to the town. We followed the miles-long line of cars through the town looking at the displays on the houses and businesses there. The children were hungry but still fascinated by the lights. I asked Anderson to pull over to get the girls something to eat and let them walk around to see the displays. He refused.

The traffic slowed to a stop. I jumped out of the car. He followed me. We fought each other right in the middle of the road and stopped traffic. No police came. No one ran to assist me. It was as if this was normal to see two people fighting in the middle of the street like it was part of the brightly lit displays. Afterwards, we got into the car as if nothing happened and returned home. I never asked him to take us to see the lights again.

∞

The war ended in 1975. We'd been pulling our troops out for a couple of years by then, but the last American deaths occurred just before the fighting stopped. Approximately 58,148 Americans died in Vietnam. Including civilians, about five million Vietnamese were killed in the war. I remember hearing the news that it was finally over. People across the country had been protesting for years, on the streets, on college campuses, in front of the White House. "Make Love, Not War," "I'd Rather Save My Ass Than Johnson's Face," and "PEACE" were some of the popular sayings of the time. When the end came though, people were more somber than joyful. There had been too much death, and no gains that people could identify, much less celebrate. The only excitement I could recall was when the soldiers started coming back home by the thousands, survivors hugging their wives and meeting their children, sometimes for the first time.

The airport scenes on television always brought me to tears. On the one hand, I was happy for them. They'd survived a battle that many thousands had lost. They could finally move forward with their lives together as a family, never worrying about when or if their husband or father was going to be brought back in one of those black bags that everyone feared, stacked by the hundreds in the cargo holds of planes, where no living being would dare be caught.

But on the other hand, I felt bad for them. So many of them believed in all their joy and excitement that the war was truly over, when for their families, it had only just begun. Wives and children would wake up so many nights, as I had, watching their husbands and fathers crawling down hallways, crouching in corners, wild-eyed and saying things that made no sense. Some of them were beaten or killed, mistaken for the Viet Cong, or as enemy informants. Unable to escape their own nightmares and flashbacks or to live a normal life again, many of the men just gave up altogether, shooting themselves in the head, or hanging themselves in their own homes.

As a nation, we were all beginning to realize that wars could never be truly won. Regardless of the outcome, we all had to pay, and the price was proving far higher than anyone could've imagined.

I also suffered my last casualty in 1975, another miscarriage. Another boy. This time, the doctor knew it was coming. He'd examined me in July, and told me to just keep taking care of myself. He left town without telling me the baby had stopped growing.

When he finally told me after the miscarriage, I asked him how he could've kept that from me.

"There was a dead baby inside of you," he said, grabbing both my hands. "If I had told you then, you would've panicked, and you may have died with him. We needed to let nature take its course. That's just life."

I was making supper in the kitchen one night in August, when the water came rushing out of me. I dropped my spoon, and clung to the stove. The pain was swift and sharp. I started to feel dizzy.

"Anderson," I called out to the bedroom, too familiar with this routine, "I got to go to the hospital. Something's wrong with the baby."

The girls were at my parents' house, so I called over there and told Mama to keep them there. I hung up the phone and I leaned against the wall. The room was spinning.

"Anderson!"

He came out of the bedroom, looking at me and the puddle on the floor. He looked around, confused, and then grabbed his keys and ran out the door.

"What're you doing?" I called him, but he was already in the car driving down the driveway.

I hobbled out the door and down the steps.

"You forgetting something, Anderson."

He put on the brakes and stared back at me, as if waking from a dream.

"Err... c'mon, get in the car," he yelled out, finally realizing his mistake. "You always causing problems."

I waddled down the driveway and into the passenger's seat, the world dimming around me. Slowly, I felt myself slip away.

When I came to, I was in a hospital bed, the room still spinning. It felt like I'd been hit by a train. When the doctor came in to make his rounds, he smiled at me, relieved.

I'd been in and out of consciousness for four days, he told me. When I arrived at the hospital, my blood pressure had dropped so low that I went into shock. They had to give me blood after they took the baby out. He'd been worried that I wasn't going to come back from it.

"Your father's here to see you," he said finally. "Do you want him to come in now?"

I nodded, too exhausted to speak.

He'd been waiting for hours. I could tell from his eyes that he hadn't slept much. He grabbed my hand and sat down. We prayed and then sat quiet, dazed. After about an hour, the nurse came in to check on me.

"Everything's looking normal, Mrs. Anderson. Your husband's here now. You want me to send him in?"

I looked over at Daddy. He nodded slowly, his face blank. He stood up, squeezed my hand, and gave me a kiss on my forehead.

"I'll be back in to see ya tomorrow." He put his hat on and walked out.

I barely looked up when Anderson walked in the room. I couldn't stand the sight of him. I was filled, at that point, with a kind of hate that I'd never experienced before, and have never since. He'd almost finished me. He'd taken two of my babies, his own sons. He'd destroyed our peace, all the love I had for him, and my body. Every trip I'd made to the emergency room, every migraine I felt, was his doing. It was sport for him, torturing me and traumatizing our daughters. He laughed when we cried, and lashed out at our happiness. I'd tried everything, prayer, pleading, kindness, flattery, even counseling. But when I told him that I'd made the appointment with the minister who married us, a man whom Anderson knew well and who I thought he respected, he told me that if that man showed up at my house, he'd be ready with two bullets—one for the minister, and one for me.

I saw him walking toward the bed, the anger in his eyes. Someone had told him it was a boy.

He reached under my sheet and pinched my leg so hard I was in too much pain to scream. He leaned toward my ear.

"Another boy, huh? I know you doing this on purpose, letting my sons die while those niggas' girls live. I'ma show you something when you get home. You betta believe it." He squeezed my leg harder for a few more seconds, then let go and walked out of the room.

Before his uncle died in 1968, he told Anderson that he desperately wanted him to have a male child, someone who could carry on the family name. As he left the room that day, I could only think that God was punishing him. Painful as it was for me, God knew that he didn't deserve a son, that he was incapable of raising a man better than himself. It was a bitter victory, but a victory nonetheless.

∞

Nineteen seventy-five was the year I decided that my war was over. There was no last straw, no final fight or argument that sent me over the edge. It was a matter of becoming too fed up, too angry, too beaten down, and partly, too old to fight anymore. I was in my late thirties,   still young, but too old to live much longer if he kept beating me. I knew it before any doctor said it. I looked in the mirror at myself shortly after leaving the hospital, just counting the bruises, none of them allowed to heal before the next attack. I'd forgotten how my skin looked without them.

I didn't want to hate him anymore. As much as I hated it for them, he was my children's father. Even if he wanted nothing to do with them, I still needed to be at peace with that fact. They were as much a part of him as they were of me.

I did it, though, mostly for my girls. I couldn't let them see me this way forever—beaten, broken, resigned to death. As Priscilla and Lisa entered high school and the boys started calling, I realized that more than to myself, I had a responsibility to them to show them a different life than what I'd been living, to let them know that relationships, marriages, are meant to build them up, not destroy them.

And so gradually, I began working toward my freedom.

In all, it took four years. I had my doubts, of course. I barely slept at night, terrified that he knew what I was up to and would finish me off before I could get away. I told no one, not my daughters, not my parents. I found a lawyer in Columbia who walked me through the process. It was more common by that time, women leaving their husbands. And I learned that, thanks to the work women had done and were doing for equal rights. I had far more options than I could ever have imagined. Property, money, custody of my girls. Freedom.

"Ma'am," the attorney said, reaching out for my hand, "you're gonna be safe now. I promise you, I'm gonna make sure of it."

∞

We continued living together and I acted no differently than any other day. I would help the children get ready for school and go to work hoping he had no clue what I was doing. My attorney told me he needed proof of the beatings. On my lunch break I went to a local department store and purchased a small tape recorder. For four years, I recorded the beatings and fights. Although he searched my belongings when I left the house, he never had a clue. I would take the recorder and tapes to my parents' house and hide them in the wall behind a bedroom dresser until I needed them.

Once he almost caught me. I knew when he walked into the house, his eyes full of fire, there was going to be a fight. He was quiet until after dinner when I hurried the girls to their rooms. I walked to the kitchen sink to wash dishes and wham, a fist to the face. I shouldn't have been caught off guard but I was. I looked around for an escape. I managed to block his next swing and ran past him to the bedroom, slamming the door behind me. This gave me time to pull out the recorder and press record. I was on my knees sliding the recorder under the bed when the door swung open. I was sure he saw what I was doing and braced for the extra beating he would give me. He came at me with all the rage he had for years. I prepared myself for the hits and screamed for him to stop. I kept on screaming until he got tired and walked out of the room. I managed to maintain enough of my sanity to retrieve the recorder and tape. I hid them in my coat pocket ready to leave when I left the house.

The day came when my attorney felt we had enough evidence against Anderson and he prepared the paperwork for a restraining order and legal separation. I went about my day as normal, going to work hoping he would not be home when I got back. I received a frantic phone call from my attorney. A man had killed his wife in town and he was afraid it was me.

We delayed the action for two weeks.

When the restraining order first came, he laughed in my face.

"What you think they gonna do? I own you. They can't keep me away from you."

The judge handling my case warned him if he didn't leave, he would put out a warrant for his arrest. The police gave him five days to get out of the house. Still, he was defiant.

"This is *my* house," he growled at me. "I'm not going nowhere, and neither are you."

At the end of the week, by the grace of God, he moved out of the house.

During our separation process, my lawyer told the judge everything that Anderson had done to me, the beatings, the rape, the endangerment of our children. He went on and on until the judge held his hand up and stopped him, because he'd heard way more than he needed to make a decision. I kept the house and the girls, and he had to pay enough to make us comfortable every month.

Afterwards, Anderson told me if he'd done everything to me that the lawyer said he did, he was sorry.

If.

I walked out of the courtroom that day in 1979 feeling lighter and younger than I had in decades. But I was still afraid. I'd spent my entire adult life under the heel of someone hell bent on destroying me, who almost did destroy me. I wasn't sure I deserved this release, this escape. I thought about the others, like Minnie, who'd suffered before me for their entire lives, about the women who were still suffering, those who wouldn't survive their husbands. And I felt the same guilt I'd felt that year Anderson was in Vietnam, when I was happy and singing Christmas carols in Mama's house. I recalled Hattie's face, sympathetic, all knowing, and what she said to me.

"Freedom is a good thing, Mae."

Freedom *is* a good thing.

Chapter 10

HE STILL SHOWS UP on Sunday mornings, eight o'clock, just as I am getting ready for church. In twenty-five years, I have never once just opened the door. Never. Even though I know he is there, I always call out, "Who is it?" And every time he gives me the same answer from the front door, the same reply he's given me since we were divorced, "It's not your nigga'."

I ignore this, as I have learned to do over the past forty years, but it still gets under my skin. It's not so much the lie as the intent. He intended for me to be guilty. I don't know exactly what he believes, but he's convinced himself that he was betrayed somehow, that it was me who made him do what he did to me daily. It still makes me furious. But still, I open the door.

By some standards, he had aged wonderfully, handsome. It's funny how those who do such ugly things to others can come away looking almost untouched. It wasn't because I didn't fight back; I became a monster. Facing him was like bristling up to a gorilla. Even though I knew his breath alone could knock me down, I still bristled up. That was the only way I knew to survive.

He'd step in the house and say a quick hello. His hands in his pockets, as usual. They'd never come out unless he needed to eat, open a door, or to gesture with his right hand while he talked. He'd smile and laugh a lot. You'd never know just how dangerous he could be.

Yes, he looked good dressed in his suit and tie ready for church, but he hasn't gone unchanged. This much I do know. He needs me now more than I ever needed him. Bill Anderson is the father of my children and so I am civil, but by no means dependent. I let him into my house because despite everything, I forgave him. There was no other way for me to move on, no other way to live a peaceful, independent life.

And I am not afraid anymore.

Our conversations were normal. We talked about work, our children, the weather, about church. He has asked me to come back to him twice. I told him that if he could give me three good reasons why I should, then I would do it. And if he could give me just one, I would take him to Paris, all expenses on me.

He has never been able to come up with one.

The offer still stands.

∞

I know war. My life had been marked at its significant points by America's fights with its so-called foreign enemies. I was born on the brink of World War II. I was married a few years after the Korean War. I had all three of my children while America fought its battle in Vietnam. And as Iraq burned, I decided it was time to speak up about the second war, the one that's been left out of the history books. The war replayed at home and the battle scars that remain unhealed.

There are no records or memorials of the lives abused or destroyed through violence in post-war homes. But those people are also casualties. Not because they volunteered to be heroes for their country, but because their country has never fully understood or cared enough about the nature of war. The only good to be gained from my experience, is sharing the knowledge that war was never victorious. There are no winners because wars never end on the battlefield; they invade and destroy the minds of the soldiers who carry that destruction back to the places that once represented peace. And as I've learned, a household, a family, a marriage without peace is lost.

There is an aftermath to this war. It shows on the faces and in the relationships of my children. Not having a good example at home, their lives have been marred by traumatic experiences, not like mine, but traumatic just the same. Sometimes I blamed myself for staying so long in a place that could have killed me, them or both, leaving behind only good memories of the days when I was not with him and my children were happy. But I know people would only talk about death and not the life, the smiles, the hope we had.

God spared us.

Many nights I prayed for the lives of our men and women in the military. I pray for their families and hope none experience what I went through. Often, I think of the smiling young man who was so eager to go into the military to be able to take care of his family and am saddened by the animal the military sent back to me.

I don't dread Sunday mornings. I don't look forward to them, either. It took me a while to understand why he even cared to come back. I was never his friend, never his lover. He retired from teaching at the technical college several years ago, but he stayed active, a proud member of the Masons and the Shriners. He had always loved institutions of brotherhood and male solidarity. I think that it may be the only thing he ever loved. Still, I think he came back because at the end of every day, despite that brotherhood, when everyone else went home to their wives, children, their grandchildren, he went home to no one. So, he thought he'd just come back after I told him that I'd forgiven him, thought he'd be able to work it out so that he could be more like them, or at least appear to be like the old him.

But I can never go back to what we had. I refuse to go back. The best I can do is open my door for him on Sundays, and answer the questions he asks about my family and the girls. Every now and then he'll see our girls, all grown, college educated, and with their own healthy families. They're all friendly with him, and invite him to family reunions, picnics, birthday parties. Sometimes he goes and sometimes he doesn't, which is just fine with them. They too have made their peace with him.

Neither of us remarried. I can't speak to why he hasn't, but I think I've just enjoyed my freedom a bit too much to get myself caught up with another man. I envy my friends sometimes; they've grown old with their husbands and the love is still there as it has always been. You can feel it when they enter a room. But I've found love in other ways—in my work at church, feeding the hungry, visiting the sick, working with patients at the doctor's office where I've been an administrator for 42 years now. But mostly I have found love in counseling young women about what love is and isn't, and how to know the difference. That's what I pray for every night—that none of the young women I meet will ever have to learn that lesson as I did.

If you are one of the millions of women who are in an abusive relationship, please seek help right away. Call the National Domestic Violence Hotline at 1-800-799-7233 to find resources and discuss your options. Their caring experts are available 24/7 to speak with you confidentially.

Veterans suffering from PTSD can get help by contacting the Veterans Crisis Line, 1-800-273-8255

ABOUT THE AUTHOR

Mary McClurkin is a retired medical office administrator who lives in South Carolina. She is a mother, grandmother and great-grandmother. She is active in her church and volunteering in her community. This is her first novel.

www.facebook.com/marymcclurkin

www.marymcclurkin.com

Twitter@readmarymac

Made in the USA
Columbia, SC
14 February 2018